100%. WOLF

by JAYNE LYONS

with illustrations by VICTOR RIVAS

 Atheneum Books for Young Readers
atheneum   NEW YORK LONDON TORONTO SYDNEY NEW DELHI

atheneum

An imprint of Simon & Schuster Children's Publishing Division • 1230 Avenue of the Americas, New York, New York 10020 • This book is a work of fiction. Any references to historical events, real people, or real places are used fictitiously. Other names, characters, places, and events are products of the author's imagination, and any resemblance to actual events or places or persons, living or dead, is entirely coincidental. • Text © 2008 by Jayne Lyons • Cover illustration © 2019 by Flying Bark Productions Pty. Ltd., Screenwest (Australia) Ltd., Create NSW, De-Fi Media Ltd., Siamese Pty. Ltd. and Screen Australia • Interior illustrations copyright © 2008 by Victor Rivas • Cover design © 2020 by Simon & Schuster, Inc. • Text originally published in Australia in 2008 by Random House Australia Pty Ltd. Publishing by arrangement with Random House Australia Pty Ltd. • All rights reserved, including the right of reproduction in whole or in part in any form. • ATHENEUM BOOKS FOR YOUNG READERS is a registered trademark of Simon & Schuster, Inc. Atheneum logo is a trademark of Simon & Schuster, Inc. • For information about special discounts for bulk purchases, please contact Simon & Schuster Special Sales at 1-866-506-1949 or business@simonandschuster.com. • The Simon & Schuster Speakers Bureau can bring authors to your live event. For more information or to book an event, contact the Simon & Schuster Speakers Bureau at 1-866-248-3049 or visit our website at www.simonspeakers.com. • Also available in an Atheneum Books for Young Readers hardcover edition • The text for this book was set in New Century Schoolbook. • The illustrations for this book were rendered in pen and ink. • Manufactured in the United States of America • 1120 OFF • First Atheneum Books for Young Readers movie tie-in paperback edition December 2020 • 10 9 8 7 6 5 4 3 2 1 • The Library of Congress has cataloged the hardcover edition as follows: Lyons, Jayne. • 100% wolf / Jayne Lyons ; illustrated by Victor Rivas.—1st ed. • p. cm. • Summary: At the time of his first transformation, a young werewolf of noble and proud ancestry is driven from his pack when, instead of turning into a fierce wolf, he changes into a little black poodle. • ISBN: 978-1-4169-7474-1 (hardcover) | ISBN 978-1-4424-0252-2 (pbk) | ISBN 978-1-5344-6700-2 (media tie-in pbk) | ISBN 978-1-4169-8262-3 (eBook) • [1. Werewolves—Fiction. 2. Poodles—Fiction. 3. Dogs—Fiction. 4. Humorous stories.] I. Rivas, Víctor, ill. II. Title. III. Title: One hundred percent wolf. IV. Title: 100 percent wolf. • PZ7.L99554Aag 2009 • [Fic]—dc22 2008052331

for Googie

CONTENTS

CHAPTER ONE:
FREDDY LUPIN

A werewolf is only actually a *wolf* for one night each month, when the moon is full. Anyone can tell when a wolf is a wolf, but how exactly do you spot a *boy* who is a wolf? That is the challenge for a wolf hunter, as Dr. Foxwell Cripp would tell anyone who would listen to him (which wasn't many people).

One clue is to look for hairs growing in the palm of the hand. Frederick Poncenby Lupin had them. Right there, a little black tuft in the middle of each palm. Frederick was called Freddy by most people, but not by his uncle. He called Freddy "that foolster Frederick!"

His uncle was the terrifying (and *very* hairy) Sir Hotspur Lupin, mayor of Milford. He was also the Grand Growler and High Howler of the Hidden Moonlight Gathering of Werefolk. In other words, he was the most pompous and powerful werewolf in Britain, and he couldn't look at Freddy without becoming purple with anger.

Sir Hotspur liked everything to be just so. Freddy was always doing and saying the wrong thing whenever his uncle was around. And just as often when he wasn't. Just last month he had accidentally put superglue on his uncle's hairbrush. It was a mistake anybody could have made.

"It wasn't me, anyway," Freddy had tried to lie. Sir Hotspur wasn't fooled. Nor did he see the funny side of walking around for a week with a hairbrush stuck to his head. Freddy, on the other hand, had seen the funny side so much that he had lain down on the floor, banged his fist, and cried with laughter. He had of course been banished to his room for the rest of the day. Again.

"You, sir, are a foolster!" Uncle Hotspur bellowed. "You will bring shame upon the Werepack of Lupin. If you don't transform into the world's most ridiculous werewolf one day, I'll eat my trousers. Eat 'em, sir!"

Relations with Uncle Hotspur had never been good. They were about to become much, much worse as tensions in Farfang Castle began to rise. For the moon was waxing toward a perfect full bright circle in the black sky and Freddy Lupin's wolf blood was warming. His first Transwolfation was approaching, and Freddy couldn't wait.

At last! Tonight the April moon would be full.

"Where are you, little pink piggies? Wolfie is coming," Freddy called as he ran.

It was a Saturday, and the morning of his one hundred and twenty-fifth birthday. (In Wolfen time, each full moon is counted. It would be about ten years and one month for a human pup.) He had already run around the house three times, shouting triumphantly.

The "house" was in fact a castle—Farfang Castle, the home of the Lupin Pack. It was an ancient building, three stories high and complete with battlements, a tower, and a moat. Across the moat was a wooden bridge where a draw-bridge had once stood. Farfang was very grand, but to Freddy it was just home. The castle was surrounded by perfect lawns and rose gardens, beyond which was a dense wood. A high stone wall and gates protected the grounds from unwanted eyes, eyes that might see things to make their owner's hair stand on end.

Sometimes a visitor (who of course knew the Lupins only as a respectable family and not as *wolves*) was invited to visit the mayor. After entering the large front door, visitors found themselves in the Great Hall, the walls of which were covered with spears, swords, stags' heads, and tapestries. On their tour they found that the castle was a square, with an open courtyard and an ornamental fountain at the center. On the far side of the castle was the kitchen, and next to it a narrow stone corridor that led to the tower. At the top of this tower, as far from the grandest rooms as was possible, was Freddy's bedroom, to which Uncle Hotspur never took anyone at all. It was the very one to which he regularly banished his annoying nephew.

"I'm going to find you, piggies. I know you took my chocolate!" Freddy yelled again.

He charged up the servants' staircase, which

led from the kitchen up to the main bedrooms, but he couldn't find the Pukesome Twosome anywhere.

The Pukesome Twosome were Uncle Hotspur's twin nine-year-old children: Harriet, a girl, and Chariot, a boy. They were the Disgusting Duo, the Putrid Pair. Freddy couldn't stand them. They were always sneaking and snitching around. They couldn't resist playing snide tricks on him, and *he* was the one who always ended up getting caught and grounded by Sir Hotspur. But Freddy had one advantage over them: One day he would transform into a werewolf but they would not. (It will be explained soon why that was so.) The twins could never be wolves—not now, not ever. It was a fact that made Sir Hotspur fume. It made the twins' eyes go narrow with envy. And it was making Freddy grin with delight, for the day that would become his Great Night was here at last.

As any werepup can tell you, the full moon on your one hundred and twenty-fifth birthday is the most exciting night of your life. It is the night of the Grand Growling, the High Howling. The night of the Hidden Moonlight Gathering of

Werefolk and the Blood Red Hunt. Most important for Freddy, it was the night of his Transwolfation, when he would become a wolf for the first time. He was going to show his uncle and the Putrid Pair that he was a wolf to be feared and admired.

Right at that moment, however, all he wanted was his chocolate back.

Freddy ran past his cousins' bedrooms on the second floor, toward the front of the castle, and arrived at the Red Stairs to take his usual shortcut. This was the grand staircase, which swept down in a curve to the center of the Great Hall. The stairs earned their name hundreds of years ago, when they had run red with blood during the Battle of Farfang Castle in 1396. The feats of Freddy's ancestor Sir Rathbone de Lupinne as he fought off his enemies were famous among werefolk. In human form, he had defeated twenty men in order to save his pack. His bloody victory was recorded in a tapestry that hung on the Great Hall's main wall. The actual suit of armor Sir Rathbone had worn on that brave day stood at the top of the stairs. The hollow metal glove still held his heavy sword. Legend said that one day the sword would once again save werefolk from destruction. But Freddy wasn't thinking about legends at that moment, only chocolate. He almost knocked the armor over as he barged past. He sat on the banister rail and slid down at high speed.

"Freddy the Fearless flies again," he bellowed as he shot down the rail. At the bottom he took off through the air and landed smack in the center of Sir Hotspur's large stomach, which, with its owner, happened to be passing. The stomach gave a mighty belch and Sir Hotspur fell backward.

"Groof!" cried Freddy's uncle as he landed heavily on his backside. The sheets of his morning newspaper flew around his head.

"It wasn't me!" Freddy immediately cried out, looking around for an excuse. He couldn't see anything or anybody else to blame. "Whoops!" he whispered to himself and bit his lip. Uncle Hotspur was still searching for breath. "Sorry," Freddy added nervously when he saw there was no escape.

He tried to help his uncle rise by pulling on the sleeve of his jacket. Sir Hotspur bashed him away with a rolled-up section of newspaper.

"Step away, sir! Meddlesome menace," cried Sir

Hotspur. "I'll be a pickled fish if you have any of Sir Rathbone's blood in your veins, sir. Pickled, I say!"

Freddy sighed. He was sick of hearing about how little he resembled Sir Rathbone. He tried to collect the sheets of newspaper that lay all over the floor, but he picked them up just as his uncle stood on them, and they tore into shreds. He handed the mess over with what he hoped was a charming smile.

The hairs on Sir Hotspur's palms shivered with annoyance as he clambered to his feet. He snatched the pieces of paper and his nostrils flared. His long red mustache trembled as he pointed at Freddy.

"I'll have no flying through the air in this castle," he gasped angrily. "No sliding, running, or leaping!"

"And no fun," Freddy said under his breath.

"What's that?" his uncle roared.

"Nothing." Freddy tried to look innocent.

"You'd better pull up your socks, boy, if you ever mean to be a wolf," Sir Hotspur growled, shaking his head.

Freddy bent down and pulled up his socks.

"How's that?" He beamed.

His uncle snarled. But before he could reply, there was a loud bang on the oak front door.

"Lord and Lady Whitehorn!" Sir Hotspur cried, instantly forgetting his irritating nephew. He was delighted that so many important werefolk would be attending the High Howling in Farfang Castle. He thrust the tattered paper at Freddy and went to welcome his guests.

"Get up to your room and stay out of my way!" he called back over his shoulder. "I'll have no foolster ruining my Great Night."

"It's *my* Great Night, actually," Freddy muttered under his breath, puffing out his belly and doing a rather good impression of his uncle's fat stomach. He was quite happy to go to his room upstairs, however. He had no intention of wasting the day meeting dull old bores who did nothing more than sit around being amazed at how much he had grown.

Freddy was banished to his room in the old tower on most days. Alone in his room, he would often look at a photograph of his father, Flasheart, who had died when Freddy was a small pup not quite four years old (in human time). Flasheart, who had been brave and kind, most unlike his brother Hotspur, looked back from the photograph with a smile. Freddy could remember him only a little, and his mother not at all, for she had died when he was a baby.

Flasheart's fate was a warning. Werewolves have a nasty and terrifying reputation, and though it's unfair, they must live in secret, for humans can be ignorant and suspicious. Some, like the dreaded Dr. Foxwell Cripp, can be downright dangerous. It was he who had discovered that Freddy's father was a werewolf and shot him with a silver bullet. Every werepup listened in terror to tales of the evil Dr. Cripp.

Freddy stood in front of his mirror and held up the photograph. He looked at his father and then at himself. They both had green eyes and strangely spiky, totally uncontrollable black hair. Their ears stuck out a little. Freddy flexed his nonexistent muscles and posed like a great warrior.

"I'm going to be a great werewolf too, Dad, just like you," Freddy told the photograph. "And you'll be proud of me because . . . because . . ."

He couldn't think of a good reason, and for a moment he began to worry. Perhaps Uncle

Hotspur was right about him. He wished his father were with him on his Great Night; he was a little frightened of his Transwolfation. He gathered his courage again, leaped onto his bed, and cried defiantly, "You *will* be proud, Dad, because tonight Freddy the invincible, the fearsome, the heroic . . . will transform!"

It was going to be the greatest night of his life.

"The mighty blood of Sir Rathbone, werewolf hero, runs through my veins," he declared. "Well, it *does*!" he added, as if trying to convince someone.

He looked at the photograph once again. He *could* be as brave as his father, he was sure of it.

"So, Uncle Hotspur, get ready . . . to eat your trousers! Eat 'em, sir!"

He laughed and flopped onto his back. Staring at the ceiling, a great notion struck him.

"With ketchup on! Because I'm going to be a great wolf."

CHAPTER TWO:
THE SLIDE OF DOOM

Now and then, throughout history, werefolk have married humans. As a result, some children—called Fangen—will transform into wolves, but others are almost human and will not. They are called Weren. There were four Fangen in Freddy's werepack: Freddy, his father, Uncle Hotspur, and Aunt Helda (who had heard the Final Howl years before). Harriet and Chariot were Weren; their palms were perfectly pink and smooth, and they would never transform. There are no rules about who will or won't become wolves. Freddy's mother had been completely human, and Freddy would experience the Transwolfation. The twins' parents had both been wolves, yet they would not. It just happens that way, but Sir Hotspur saw it as a personal humiliation. The fact that it was Freddy inheriting the Fangen blood was an even greater insult.

"It's an outrage!" Sir Hotspur had roared only yesterday, glaring at Freddy, who had just walked dog dirt over every carpet in the castle. Freddy had been playing with a stray dog that had somehow found a way onto the grounds. This was very unusual, for normally dogs avoided Farfang Castle in terror. He had fed the animal, but didn't notice that he'd stepped in the stray's *number two*. He was standing in front of his outraged uncle with the poo still on his shoe before he realized.

"But it was hungry . . . ," Freddy tried to explain. The poor animal had fled at the smell of his furious uncle.

"It is a *dog*, sir! A dog! Not fit to be in our presence, and yet you . . ." Hotspur came to a stop. There were no words for his disgust.

"I don't see what's so wrong with dogs. After all, we're *wolves*. It's not so different. . . ."

"A wolf is a *noble* being, sir!" Uncle Hotspur's face was sweating with fury. "We are not animals! I will not have an animal in my castle, sir! Never!

Why should *you* transform? You are a foolster!"
Sir Hotspur shuddered with disgust. He hated
the fact that it was Freddy who carried the wolf
blood of Sir Rathbone in his veins and not his
own pups. Freddy, as usual, had been banished
to his room.

That was yesterday, and now—on his birthday—
Freddy was banished to his room at the top of
the tower yet *again*. And he was bored.

"Bored, bored, bored, bored, bored, bored!" he
bellowed down the spiral stairs. *"Bored!"* he
added, throwing himself onto his bed.

His TV and computer had been confiscated
the week before, as punishment for dropping
a water balloon onto his uncle's head. (He had
been aiming for Harriet, but she had outwitted
him as usual.) He had tried to read, but it was
no use—he was far too excited about the High
Howling and his Transwolfation. In the end he
had no other option. It was time to ride the Slide
of Doom.

He dragged a huge metal tray out from behind
his cupboard. It was big enough for a grown
man to sit on. Freddy had few memories of his

father, but the best was of them sitting on the tray together. Flasheart Lupin had invented the Slide of Doom when he was a boy. Freddy dragged the tray to the doorway, placed it on the floor, and sat on it. Below him the long, steep spiral staircase went all the way down to the ground floor. The ride continued fast down the passage next to the kitchen and, finally, through a doorway into the central courtyard.

Freddy sat on the tray, daring himself to push off. He had been absolutely, permanently, and totally banned from the Slide of Doom by Sir Hotspur. It was too *undignified* for a wolf, especially a Lupin. But Uncle Hotspur simply didn't know how to have fun. And anyway . . . he would never know, would he?

"Doom to boring Uncle Hotair!" Freddy pushed off with a cry of delight.

He held the tray's handles tightly as the metal sheet shot down over the ancient stone steps. His straight black hair stood on end with the speed of the ride, and his grin was enormous. Not even his sticky-out ears could slow him down. The curves were so tight that Freddy went round and round like bathwater shooting down a drain.

"Yoo-woo!" he howled. "Fantabulous!"

Then, as usual, everything went wrong.

Freddy shot out of the bottom of the staircase straight toward Sir Hotspur and Lord and Lady Whitehorn, who were being given a grand tour of the castle.

"Look out!" yelled Freddy.

"Let me save you, Lady Whitehorn!" cried Sir Hotspur, picking up the tiny lady chivalrously.

Too late!

Freddy whacked into his uncle for the second time in one day. Sir Hotspur fell back onto the tray, knocking Freddy off and letting out a great "Gr-oomf!" as Lady Whitehorn landed on his lap. The pair flew down the corridor toward the courtyard, looking rather surprised.

A little scream came from Lady Whitehorn as she and Sir Hotspur shot out of the open door and came to rest in the ornamental pond with a small splash. A stone fountain shaped like a boy peed water onto Sir Hotspur's furious red face. Lady Whitehorn threw a goldfish off her lap with a growl.

"I had no wish for a swim, Lupin!"

"Whoops . . . ," Freddy croaked. Nobody could

be in more trouble than he was at that precise moment. "Well, actually, you're supposed to steer left at the last minute," he instructed helpfully, "or else you end up in the pond."

"I'm going to mash you, sir. Mashed like a potato, boiled and peeled. I'll serve you up for dog food. I'll . . . I'll . . ." Sir Hotspur stood in the pond, pointing a finger at his nephew and looking more than half wolf already. Freddy didn't wait for his uncle to carry out his potato threats. He sprinted back up to his tower room as fast as he could and dived under his bed in a rather unheroic manner.

Freddy soon heard angry footsteps climbing the stairs. "Great howls," he croaked. What would his uncle do now?

"Well, what do you have to say for yourself, young man?"

Freddy sighed with relief when he heard it was only Mrs. Mutton, the housekeeper, coming up to see him. She was a Weren and had looked after him for as long as he could remember. She had adored Flasheart, and she had a very big soft spot for Freddy and no time at all for Sir

Hotspur, who was actually a little afraid of the fat old lady. She could always be relied on to stick up for Freddy against his horrid uncle. This time, however, Freddy did not come out from under the bed.

"Old Hotair says you must stay in your room until midnight," Mrs. Mutton informed the dark space under the bed.

"But that's not fair. I'll miss my party. *Ouch!*" Freddy hit his head on the bed as he jumped with fury.

"Freddy Lupin! The most important werefolk in Britain will be there. You can't be trusted to behave yourself," she said crossly.

"Well, actually, I can. Can, can, can, can!" he grumbled. "I always behave myself. *Actually*. It's not my fault that everything goes wrong."

Mrs. Mutton snorted an incredulous laugh. "Remember, young pup, it's not just *your* party tonight. It's a blue moon next month, and so the Fang Council will be discussing the reelection of the Grand Growler. Hotspur's sure to win again, but he won't trust you not to ruin everything."

"Humph," replied Freddy. "It's not my fault he can't steer. Dad could do it."

"I bet Lady Whitehorn is already too cross to vote for him." The old lady smiled.

Freddy couldn't help but laugh too.

"What would your father say about tipping your uncle into the pond?" the housekeeper demanded, peering under the bed.

"Good shot!" Freddy answered.

Mrs. Mutton looked at the ceiling in despair.

"It's your first Transwolfation tonight, Freddy," she continued seriously. "It's time to stop behaving like a foolish pup and think about what you owe to your family. To the memory of your father, and to Sir Rathbone."

Freddy went silent as his stomach started to churn with nerves.

"It's time to grow up, pup, and think of others! As much as I hate to admit it, Sir Hotair does a great job as Grand Growler. You must behave yourself tonight."

Freddy closed his eyes. He was half ecstatic about the night to come and half terrified.

"Well, Freddy," Mrs. Mutton sighed when he didn't answer. "Happy birthday. If you won't come out, I'll send your present in." With that, she slid a nicely wrapped present under the bed and her footsteps disappeared down the stairs again.

Freddy unwrapped it eagerly.

"An Ultra Thousand Taser DS-Boy?! Fanta-bulous!" It was exactly what he had wanted—the most cutting-edge console game in the world. Mrs. Mutton was the best ever.

Freddy squirmed out from under his bed to thank the old lady and flung open his bedroom door. Suddenly he was flying, but not in a good way.

"Arrggh!" he cried as he sprawled through the air and fell down the top few steps. The Ultra Thousand Taser DS-Boy fell from his grasp and clattered down and down the spiral stairs. He looked back in fury to see Harriet and Chariot smiling at him evilly, holding a piece of rope stretched across his doorway.

"Enjoy your trip, Fred-er-ick-*smell-of-sick*?" sang the twins happily.

"You could have killed me!" Freddy yelled in outrage.

"As if we'd be so lucky," Harriet snorted. "You're in trouble now, dunderbrain."

"Who asked *you*, piggy?"

Harriet ignored him and breezed into his room.

"Hey, stay out!" Freddy cried, struggling to rise as Chariot followed his sister.

Both the twins had tiny blue eyes and red hair, like their father. They were pink and plump like two piglets, a fact that Freddy was always cruelly happy to point out. They never ran, shouted, skidded, or burped; never farted at the dinner table or spoke with their mouths full; never wiped snot on their sleeves, flew down the banister into Sir Hotspur's stomach, or sent Lady Whitehorn into the pond. In fact, they never did any of the things Freddy did that drove his uncle wild.

"You put that down! That's private property," Freddy cried in fury as Harriet picked up the photograph of his father. It was usually hidden when they were around.

The twins' eyes flashed wide with delight as they looked at each other. They had discovered a new torture for their cousin.

Freddy tried to grab the photograph from Harriet, but she jumped onto the bed and dangled it out of reach. Just as he almost caught her, Chariot took the photograph and stuck his hand out the window.

"Does Freddy-Sicky want his daddy?" he taunted. "Will he cry-ee?"

"Give it back, fart-breath, or you'll be sorry!" Freddy demanded as he made a lunge for the photograph.

"Bye-bye, Daddy . . . ," Chariot said as he let the photograph fall. The twins babbled with laughter as it caught on the wind and flew away.

"That was a"—Freddy couldn't think of a word bad enough—"despicagusting thing to do."

The twins continued laughing.

"Putrid pink pair!" Freddy shouted, picking up a pillow. He chased them onto the staircase and began to aim blows at them.

"Oh, help!" scoffed Harriet. "A pillow? You are so totally not scary."

"You'll never be a wolf like my dad," taunted Chariot.

"No, I won't!" raged Freddy. "I won't be *fat and mean and cowardly* like your dad. I'll be a hero like Sir Rathbone and brave like *my* dad. At midnight you'll see! I'll make you shiver in your shoes, piggies. Look what's happening."

Freddy held up his hand. The twins stopped

laughing as the hairs on his palm twitched and curled over.

"See? I'm getting ready," Freddy said with a gleam in his eye. He dropped his voice to an icy whisper. "My blood is getting warmer. And when it's red-hot, I'll look at the moon and . . . Yooo-wooo! That's when you'll see I am one hundred percent wolf, not like you pathetic Weren. You'd better be hiding, too, because I'll be coming to bite your bratty backsides." Chariot opened his eyes with terror, but Harriet stuck her nose in the air and flounced down the stairs.

"Oh yes! Ha-ha-hardy-ha!" cried Freddy in triumph, aiming a final whack of his pillow at Chariot as he followed his sister. "Just wait till midnight, little piggies. This big bad wolf is going to blow your house down." He slammed his door with a flourish and then, remembering his birthday present, opened it again and ran down the stairs. The Ultra Thousand Taser DS-Boy was broken into five jagged pieces.

Freddy vowed to be the most terrifying wolf in the history of Wolfenkind. He was going to teach the Pukesome Twosome a lesson they would never forget.

CHAPTER THREE:
THE HIGH HOWLING

The Grand Growler is the most important were-wolf in the country and must be descended from a noble family, for he is the guardian of the were-folk's most sacred rituals. Wolves are fiercely proud people, and it is the Grand Growler's role to ensure that the High Howling is a very special and dignified occasion. Every five years the Fang Council decides who will be elected for the next term, and for the past five hundred years, a member of the Lupin pack had always entered the election for Grand Growler. Flasheart Lupin had held the position, and after his death his brother, Hotspur, had taken his place.

Being Grand Growler was more important to Sir Hotspur than anything else in the world. He was desperate to be reelected, so it was hardly surprising that he didn't trust Freddy not to ruin everything. He had been in a total frenzy all afternoon, directing deliveries of meat and red wine, making sure that all the armor and treasure were polished until sparkling, and finding bedrooms for guests who had arrived too early. Freddy was so desperate to be reinvited to the party that he even risked going downstairs to apologize to Sir Hotspur for the dreadful pond incident. It was no use. His uncle simply did not trust him to be let loose among the guests. Instead, Freddy could only watch them arrive from his window in the tower. Mrs. Mutton, sick of Sir Hotspur's orders, was hiding up there with him.

"That's Sir Grey Hightail, leader of the Fang Council. He's the oldest wolf in the Great Pack and extremely wise. Even Hotair has to listen to him."

Mrs. Mutton was pointing down from the tower window at the castle courtyard. The guests were gathering around the pond, which was full of floating candles. It was approaching midnight, and they had seen magnificent car after magnificent car drive up to the gates. The housekeeper knew all the visitors' names. "The Snotte-Muzzels, they're Weren. Haven't had a wolf in the pack for years. They keep hoping that one of the grand-pups will transform." Mrs. Mutton shook her head in commiseration.

"Who's that?" laughed Freddy. The shortest, fattest man he had ever seen rolled into sight.

"Colonel Slimpaw. He's just as fat when he's a wolf, too." The old lady chuckled and then looked at Freddy seriously.

"All these fine werefolk are here to honor you, pup. It's you who will carry on Sir Rathbone's Fangen blood in this pack. Just remember, you come from the most ancient and noble line of wolves in Britain. Everybody will remember the name of Freddy Lupin, and his first Trans-wolfation. Your parents would have been very proud."

Freddy's heart swelled. There was nothing he wanted more than to be a heroic wolf. He gave a nervous squirm. All afternoon he had endured the most terrible itching. In the tufts of hair in his palms it was almost unbearable. The clock said ten minutes before midnight. At long last it was time!

"Ready?" Mrs. Mutton asked. He gave a nervous nod.

Dressed in his best and most uncomfortable clothes, Freddy set off for the Great Hall with the old lady. They walked down the spiral staircase from his tower room and along the narrow stone passage next to the kitchen.

"Stop wriggling, will you?" Mrs. Mutton instructed.

"I can't help it, I'm itchy," he complained, tugging at his tight collar. He felt most uneasy and his stomach still ached with excitement. They walked up the servants' staircase to the second floor. In less than five minutes he would be a wolf at last. It was everything he wanted, and yet he felt frightened, too. They walked past the bedrooms toward the front of the castle. What would the Transwolfation be like? What if it hurt? If only his father were there to talk to him. But there was no more time left to worry now. Freddy could hear the noise of the party below.

They reached the top of the Red Stairs. Below them the Great Hall was lit by candlelight, and the jeweled crowd glittered. Freddy stood next to Sir Rathbone's armor and placed a hand on it for reassurance. His stomach felt terrible, as if he were going to puke. Somebody looked up and spotted him. The most important werefolk in Britain all cheered, and, with a push from the housekeeper, Freddy began to walk down the Red Stairs into the Great Hall.

Uncle Hotspur glared menacingly at his troublesome nephew, but Freddy, finally starting to enjoy himself, waved at everybody like a pop star.

"Well done, Freddy . . ."

"Sharpen those fangs . . ."

"Break a paw . . ."

"Come on, moonbeam . . . ," came the calls.

He saw the twins, their faces sour with envy. They had been forced there to see his Great Night much against their will. He waved at them deliberately, as if they were his greatest fans. Harriet scowled at him.

Eventually Freddy worked his way to the front of the room. Sir Hotspur stood waiting grimly on a small stage, behind which was a huge curtain. He pointed at a chair with a fierce scowl.

"I'll have no buffoonery tonight!" he whispered fiercely in Freddy's ear. "You, sir, had better change into the most impressive wolf to walk the earth. The pride of the Lupin Pack depends on it, and Sir Rathbone's memory demands it."

Sir Hotspur's reelection as Grand Growler also depended on it, although that quite escaped Freddy's mind.

"Yes sir," Freddy croaked nervously, trying to look fierce.

As Sir Hotspur stood up and raised his hands, the crowd fell silent.

"Honored guests, Weren, Fangen, all! The time has come. Now is the Grand Growling and High Howling of the Hidden Moonlight Gathering of Werefolk. We howl thanks for the ancient magic of the Moonstone. Now, by the power of the silver moon, let the Transwolfation begin!"

With that, Sir Hotspur pulled back the curtain to reveal a tall window. There in the midnight sky shone a perfect, beautiful full moon. Although Freddy was standing back from the light, his skin began to itch even more. All around him, Fangen struck by the moonbeams began transforming into wolves. Large old graying wolves, young beautiful black wolves, wolves with sleek brown hair, even pure-white wolves. Lady Whitehorn transformed into a tiny pale wolf with her diamond tiara still balanced precariously on her head. It was a terrible and magnificent sight. Howling filled the air. While still a boy, Freddy couldn't understand the Wolfen words; they sounded like deadly music. Only as a wolf would he be able to join in this ancient language. Eventually all the wolves apart from Sir Hotspur and his nephew had transformed.

"Now you, Frederick," Uncle Hotspur ordered. "And make it good, sir! This is no place for a foolster," he added menacingly, his eyes glaring from under his hairy red eyebrows.

Freddy felt like running away, but he pulled together his courage and walked toward the patch of moonlight. The crowd fell silent in anticipation.

"Please don't let it hurt," Freddy whimpered to himself.

As he stepped into the moonbeams, he felt the most marvelous warmth spread over his body. The light of the moon for a Fangen is like the sun's rays on a beautiful summer day. He began to stretch, and it felt glorious, like picking a scab or scratching an itch. It was as if he were turning and twisting inside out. He fell forward onto his hands and knees, and a searing shiver shot through him as he felt new hair growing through his skin. A few moments later Freddy had transformed. He put back his head and howled with joy.

"Yip!"

Freddy opened his eyes in alarm.

The wolves howled in disgust.

The Putrid Pair squealed with delight.

Sir Hotspur roared with rage.

Freddy felt that something was not quite right. . . . He ran to the window and looked at his reflection against the dark night.

"Yip!" he woofed in shock. The reflection staring back at him was not that of a fearsome, proud wolf. Instead, he saw a perfectly tiny, utterly unfierce, and totally ridiculous black poodle.

"I'm a werepoodle!"

Never once in his nightmares had he imagined a fate as bad as this. Surely life couldn't get any worse?

Oh, poor old Freddy. Life could be, and was about to become, very much worse.

CHAPTER FOUR:
DRIPSY-WIMPSY

The room echoed with a tumult of furious howls.

There could be no sight more repulsive to werefolk than a dog in their midst. Even normal wolves and dogs distrust each other. Dogs see themselves as civilized and wolves as wild and dangerous. Since cavemen first threw sticks, dogs have always sided with men against wolves. Dogs lived in the humans' caves, then their huts, and then their houses, but wolves were always in the forests. Then wolves were gradually driven out of the ancient woods as humans built their towns. The wolves viewed the dogs, which helped men hunt them down, as traitors to animalkind.

For werefolk the disgust with dogs goes even deeper. Added to the distrust any normal wolf feels is a fear of discovery, since some humans would seek not only to drive them away, but to destroy them entirely. Not even human form will fool some dogs—some can always smell the wolf within. Sir Rathbone himself had been tracked down and uncovered by a wolfhound. These traitorous beasts had led soldiers to the gates of this very house in the Battle of Farfang Castle.

Worse than all this, for some wolves such as Uncle Hotspur, is the suggestion that a Fangen may be an *animal*. Werefolk are exceptionally proud people and cannot bear to look at a dog as it reminds them that they may not be so very different from beasts. Whatever the reason, any association with a dog is a disgrace too terrible to think about.

Freddy turned to look at his uncle in alarm. Sir Hotspur, now transformed into a huge red wolf, was approaching, his teeth bared and dripping with saliva.

"You ridiculous buffoon," he growled. "You have brought shame upon us that we will never live down. The very blood of Sir Rathbone has been polluted."

Freddy backed away in alarm. It appeared

Uncle Hotspur wouldn't be eating his trousers after all.

"I'm going to mince you into little poodle pieces. Then I'll spit them out and grind them into the floor," howled his furious, slavering uncle. Freddy watched, frozen with terror, as the monstrous wolf leaped at him.

Freddy gave a feeble yelp and ran away as fast as his tiny, pretty legs would take him. He crossed the Great Hall, and a sea of disgusted wolves howled at him as he passed.

"Shame!"

"Disgrace!"

Amid the uproar, Freddy scampered out of the Great Hall, down the passage, and up the spiral stairs to his room. There he sank down under his bed in shock, sorrow, and confusion. How could this be? How could he be a dog—the most despicable creature on earth? The son of Flasheart, a most magnificent wolf, doomed to be loathed and shunned by all werefolk. It couldn't have happened; there must be a mistake.

Freddy tippy-toed over to the mirror.

"Oh, stinking, smelly feet," he yipped in despair. There was no doubting his reflection.

He was a poodle.

"Why can't I be normal like every other were-wolf? I'm supposed to be a hero." Footsteps were approaching up the spiral stairs. "Oh, great howls!" Freddy whimpered, his hair going tight with fear. He scampered under the bed once more. To his relief, it was Mrs. Mutton who walked in and sat heavily on the bed. To his further relief, he found that he could still understand her. The Fangen could always understand humans when in wolf form, but he hadn't been so sure about himself as a *dog*.

"Well, I've never seen anything like this before," she began unhelpfully. "Your father had pure Wolfen blood. He was never a poodle, you know, not even once."

Freddy sighed. He didn't need to be reminded what a ridiculous son he was for the famously brave Flasheart. His father would have been ashamed of him for sure.

Mrs. Mutton suddenly slapped her leg in realization and peered under the bed. "I remember who you remind me of now. Dripsy-Wimpsy, of course!"

Freddy had no idea what she was talking

about. He didn't want to know; all he wanted was to wake up from this nightmare.

"Whenever your mother's aunt came to visit, she brought her dog, too. Well, you can imagine how Hotspur reacted. But Flasheart allowed the ghastly little traitor to stay here for your mother's sake. It was the sliest, smelliest, most cowardly poodle in the world. Always yipping, farting, and pooing on your uncle's lawn. You look exactly like her."

"Woof!" Freddy objected crossly. He looked nothing like a girl dog, and he wasn't farty! Well, not always. Except if he ate baked beans, or peas, or broccoli, or . . .

"Sir Hotspur is very upset," Mrs. Mutton continued.

"Yip," yelped the poodle, knowing his uncle would never forgive him. He had no wish to be minced into tiny poodle pieces, or mashed like a potato.

"If I were a poodle, which thank goodness I'm not, I'd stay up here till morning," said the old lady as she stood and walked toward the stairs. "Come down tomorrow when you're a boy again. Everything will look better soon, you'll see." As she began to descend, she called back, "Sir Hotair might even have calmed down by then."

Freddy agreed. There was no way he was coming out looking as he did. Fangen only stay in wolf form for the first night of the full moon; the next morning he would transform back into a boy and be safe from this horror until next month.

But rather than looking better for Freddy, things began to look decidedly worse just then, as the Pukesome Twosome emerged from the shadows behind the door. They had been eavesdropping.

"Woof!" Freddy, forgetting his resolution, shot out from under the bed to order them from the room.

He was snatched up by Chariot and, despite his nipping and kicking, was dumped roughly into an old sack.

"Not such a fierce wolf, are you, *Dripsy-Wimpsy*?" Harriet taunted with delight. "What a sissy."

Poor old Freddy snapped and yipped with outrage, but there was no escape. What a terrible ending to his Great Night. Not only a poodle and a national disgrace, but trapped by his archenemies.

CHAPTER FIVE:
THE MOONSTONE

"Just wait till I'm human again! I'll, I'll . . . destructionate you!" Freddy threatened from his sack. Of course, the twins had no idea what he was woofing.

"Ruffy-tuff-yip-youy?" repeated Chariot, swinging the sack through the air.

"Don't cry, Dripsy," taunted Harriet, giving the bag a bang. "We won't let Daddy find you." With a peal of laughter the twins ran down the spiral stairs. Freddy was relieved they were not taking him to Uncle Hotspur, but whatever his cousins were up to, it wasn't friendly.

Anyway, I can't stay here forever. I'll be a boy again when the sun comes up, and then nobody can keep me in a bag, he remembered thankfully.

"So watch out, because that's when I'll be after you!" he woofed menacingly at his cousins. "I'll chase you right out of Milford."

"Stop barking, dunderbrain," warned Harriet. "Do you want Daddy to find you?"

Furious but nervous, Freddy kept quiet.

Suddenly Chariot dropped the sack on the floor. They were in Harriet's bedroom on the second floor of the castle.

"Groof!" complained Freddy.

"Shush, dog-breath," his cousin hissed.

Freddy tried gnawing at the sack, but it was no use. He was well and truly stuck in the smelly old bag.

"Are you sure he has one?" Chariot asked his sister. "He could be thrown out of the Hidden Moonlight Gathering if they knew."

"I told you I saw it, didn't I?" she replied.

"Well, go and get it, then," he snapped.

Freddy heard Harriet walk out of the room. While she was gone, Chariot amused himself by pinching at Freddy through the cloth of the sack. When the poodle managed to bite his finger at last, Chariot wailed and jumped back in surprise.

"Ha-ha-hardy-ha!" Freddy woofed in triumph.

"And when I get out of this bag, I'll bite your farty backside, too!" Chariot listened nervously to the muffled woofs until he heard Harriet's rapid footsteps.

"Have you got it? Did he see you? Will it work?" he asked eagerly.

"Of course it will work, dunderbrain!" she snapped, and pulled the sack toward herself. Freddy had no idea what they were talking about, but he didn't like the sound of it.

Harriet opened the sack, and Freddy jumped out in a flash. Just as he had promised, Freddy immediately caught Chariot by the backside and bit down as hard as he could.

"Yyyooooowwwww!" cried the boy, leaping around the room. Freddy held on tightly as they raced in a circle.

"That's it, Charry, hold him," called Harriet.

She held up a thin chain made of strong metal. A small white stone in the shape of a teardrop dangled from it like a pendant. In her other hand she had a padlock. Before Freddy knew what was happening, the chain with the white stone was around his neck and the padlock was fastened tight. Freddy let go of his cousin's backside in alarm. He shook his head furiously to and fro but couldn't budge the chain. He tried using his paw to break it, but it was much too strong. He ran to a mirror and gasped in horror when he saw the small white stone gleaming back at him. He knew instantly what it was; all werefolk would have recognized it.

"A Moonstone!" howled Freddy in despair.

"A Moonstone!" howled the twins in triumph.

This was the most terrible thing that could have happened to Freddy at that moment. A Moonstone is a very rare, sacred, and *dangerous* object. No one, not even Grey Hightail, understood all its powers. It was believed that the magic of the stone had given rise to the first werefolk many thousands of years ago. Only two of its powers were known for certain. The first was that when held or worn by a normal human, the stone would become hot if a Fangen approached. Sometimes it could even warm the human's blood, which could serve as a warning. For this reason any stones known to exist were kept safely hidden by the Fang Council. If they should ever fall into the hands of an enemy, they could be used to hunt down Fangen. It was against the law of the Hidden Moonlight Gathering for any-one to possess one. The second power was that any Fangen in contact with a Moonstone could neither Transwolfate nor return to human form while in contact with the stone. As long as he wore that Moonstone, Freddy Lupin would be Dripsy-Wimpsy forever.

CHAPTER SIX:
THE BLOOD RED HUNT

"*Hoooowwwwlllll*. Boil my head if that pup is any blood of mine, sir!"

Freddy froze. There was no mistaking the howl of Uncle Hotspur coming from below. Despite his troubles, he felt a small wave of relief run over him. Not only could he still understand humans, he could understand his uncle's Wolfen words too. This proved that no matter what he looked like, he did indeed have true wolf blood in him. No ordinary dog can understand a wolf, nor a wolf a dog. It was another of the many reasons they hated and feared each other so much. But now it gave Freddy a small glimmer of hope.

His hope didn't last long. A terrifying roar

43

echoed around the castle and grew to a chorus as the visiting wolves joined in.

"Shame!"

"Shame!"

"Shame!"

The sound was appalling, even to werefolk. Harriet locked her bedroom door and looked at Chariot in alarm. Never before had the wolves sounded so angry. To have the sacred ritual of the High Howling reduced to a pantomime was a terrible thing. For the Lupin Pack, it spelled disaster. The wolves' anger, which had been growing for the past half hour, had now exploded.

Freddy hung his head in shame. It was all his fault. All he had wanted was to be a wolf to make his father proud.

Suddenly there was a tremendous commotion as a hundred sets of heavy, clawed paws thundered across the stone floor of the hall and out into the garden.

"The Hunt!" gasped Chariot, jumping to the window. Harriet joined him, and they pushed each other back and forth trying to see.

"The Blood Red Hunt," Freddy sighed.

As the newest member of the Great Pack, he should have had the honor of leading the Fangen in the Hunt. But how ridiculous would the proud wolves look being led by a silly black poodle? He couldn't even catch a mouse, let alone a deer or a fox. Freddy realized now that the Great Pack would never accept him as a member. He would be an outcast forever. He jumped sadly onto Harriet's bed to look out the other window.

Down below on the lawn was a chilling and marvelous sight: a hundred howling wolves circling and snarling in the white beams of moonlight. As Freddy watched, Uncle Hotspur shook his huge red head, opened his jaws, and snarled out to the Fangen, "I, Grand Growler and High Howler, will lead the hunt in place of that foolster, Frederick."

He leaped to the front of the pack. As he did, a large gray wolf turned to face him and bared his teeth menacingly.

"No, Lupin," growled the old wolf.

"Who's that?" Chariot whispered, pushing his sister aside.

"It's Hightail, of course!"

"Shhh!" Freddy woofed, trying to listen as the

two wolves circled each other and the children continued to argue.

"Do you dare stand in the way of the Grand Growler when he smells red blood?" snarled Sir Hotspur.

The old wolf shook his head.

"You are the Grand Growler no longer, Lupin. The Fang Council has decided. Your pup has brought shame upon the most sacred night of the Hidden Moonlight Gathering. Step aside, Hotspur."

"What are they saying?" Chariot wanted to know.

"How am I supposed to know, dunderbrain? I'm not a wolf," Harriet snapped. "Ask Dripsy-Wimpsy over there."

"But neither is he," Chariot snorted. The twins gurgled with unpleasant laughter.

At his own window Freddy nearly choked with unpleasant surprise. He understood what was being said, but now he wished he didn't. Poor Uncle Hotspur. He might be pompous and terrifying, but it was hardly his fault that Freddy was a poodle.

His uncle agreed with him. "That disgrace

Frederick is nothing to do with me!" he roared, stamping his paw. "I told Flasheart that marrying a human would bring trouble."

"Remember, Hotspur, that your own grandmother was a human. And you only became Grand Growler because your brother was shot by Cripp," Hightail replied.

At the sound of that hated name all the wolves snarled loudly.

"Flasheart was impulsive and daring," continued Hightail. "Even so, the dignity of the High Howling was always safe in *his* hands. You come from an ancient and honorable pack. Yes, Sir Rathbone saved all Wolfenkind from destruction, but this disgrace cannot be overlooked. There can be no place in the Hidden Moonlight Gathering for the Lupin Pack now. I lead the Blood Red Hunt tonight, and on the next month's blue moon the council will elect a new Grand Growler."

Sir Hotspur sat on his hind legs in shock. With a fury of snarls and howls the Blood Red Hunt streaked across the lawn and disappeared into the darkness of the woods.

Freddy watched as his uncle, alone in the moonlight, paced around in a slow circle. Freddy felt so sorry for all that had happened. Sorry that he was a poodle, that his Great Night had been ruined, that he had a Moonstone around his neck, and that he had brought disgrace to the Lupin Pack. He was even sorry for Uncle Hotspur . . . but not too much. Freddy sighed and put back his head and howled. A rather thin, not very terrifying, and quite obviously poodle-y howl.

Before he could react, the smelly sack was thrown over him once again and he was dumped roughly into Harriet's cupboard. The twins were intent on revenge, and Freddy was going to pay for his name-calling.

CHAPTER SEVEN

PAMMY'S POODLE PARLOR

The next morning, Freddy was disturbed from an exhausted and miserable sleep by the twins.

"Keep quiet, Dripsy-Wimpsy!" Harriet hissed. "Unless you want Daddy to make you into a poodle pie? He's looking everywhere for you."

Indeed, Freddy could hear his uncle, now a man again, calling for him furiously. He wisely stayed very still.

"Yeah, dog-breath. We're going for a little walk outside," warned Chariot, as he hauled the sack up.

Freddy's ears perked up at this news. As the twins carried him downstairs, he started making plans for escape. All around him were the sounds of the guests departing. Eventually, when he calculated that they must have walked outside the gates of the castle, he began to jump and scratch as hard as he could until Chariot dropped the bag. Freddy landed on the pavement with a groan.

"Stupid poodle!" the boy cried. "You've scratched me."

"Don't be such a baby," Harriet snorted.

The Putrid Pair laughed as the sack containing Freddy rolled about on the floor. It was tied tightly and there was no escape.

"Poor old Dripsy-Wimpsy," they taunted. "Dripsy by name, wimpsy by nature. Can't even get out of a bag."

Freddy howled with frustration and fury. Harriet bent down to talk to him.

"If you stop struggling, Wimpsy, we'll let you out in a minute," she promised.

"And then you'll wish you hadn't!" Freddy woofed furiously. "'Cause then I'll bite your piggy bum." He stopped jumping around nonetheless.

Chariot carefully picked up the sack once more, and the three cousins continued their walk into town. At last they entered a shop—Freddy could tell by the jingle of the bell at the door.

Inside there were some most unusual smells: the smell of dogs (which was, strangely, quite nice to his nose), but also other, terrible stinks. Freddy's human brain knew that they were the smells of . . . what? *Something familiar?* Yes . . . he had it! Shampoo, soap, and perfume. His dog nose hated those smells even more than his boy nose. To his poodle brain they stank of the very worst sort of putrid puke, the most vomitous stench. He heard the Pukesome Twosome giggling. They obviously had a nasty trick planned for him, but this time Freddy was ready. This time they would find out that it is not so easy to pick on a werewolf, even if he is a poodle.

"Good morning, twins!" sang an unfamiliar voice, a woman's. "And how is Mayor Lupin today?"

"Oh, very happy," Harriet said sweetly, "because he has a new pet dog. He's in here."

Chariot plonked the sack roughly on a table.

"Hold your nose—he stinks," he warned. "Careful he doesn't try to escape. He's such a *sissy.*"

Freddy yipped in protest.

"Don't worry, wittle doggie-woggie," the woman called out to the sack. "Evwy wittle puppy is scaredy-waredy on his first wickle visit to Pammy's Poodle Parlor."

Freddy woofed in disgust at her ridiculous baby talk. Did she think he was a puppy? Then he paused in horror.

What in wolfdom happened at *Pammy's Poodle Parlor*?

"Shall we let the bwave wittle doggie out, then?" snoodled Pam, reaching her hand out to the sack.

Freddy was on full escape alert. The second the sack was opened, he jumped out. Pam gave a shriek.

"Stinkification!" Freddy barked. The shop door was closed, and he was too small to reach the handle. He ran around the room in desperate circles looking for a way out. His little clawed toes scraped over the tiled floor as he skidded around. There was no escape! He yipped in frustration. The pink twins laughed loudly as they watched him.

"Oh, isn't he sweet?" cried Pam. "A wovely wittle poodle. What's his name?"

"Dripsy-Wimpsy," Harriet told her with an evil smile.

"How adorable!" Pam shrieked. "Come on now,

Dripsy-Wimpsy, Pammy isn't going to hurt the wittle doggie. I'm just going to make him look pwetty."

This made Freddy run even faster around the room. Nobody made a werewolf look pwetty!

"I'll get him," announced Chariot, chasing after Freddy. As they raced and lurched around, Chariot crashed into a chair and knocked over a tray of brushes.

"Oh, do be careful," Pam called out in alarm. Chariot ignored her and skidded under a table after Freddy. He caught hold of his cousin's front paw, but Freddy nipped at his fingers with a snarl.

"Youch!" yelped Chariot. He jumped up and whacked his head under the table. "*Youch!*" he bellowed once more.

Harriet was quicker than them both. She grabbed Freddy by a hind leg and dangled him in the air. It was a most undignified position for a wolf to be in. Freddy tried to bite her but couldn't reach. Pam had a muzzle over his nose and mouth in a second. She plonked him onto the tabletop and tied the muzzle's lead to a little hook on the edge of the table. Freddy was trapped again! He was furious with himself. He truly was the world's most useless werewolf.

He growled as menacingly as a poodle who was supposed to be a wolf could. One day the Putrid Pair would pay for this.

"Now then, Dripsy-Wimpsy!" Pam said, rearranging her hair. "Naughty wittle doggies don't get any doggie choc-wocs."

Freddy glared at her.

"Now for Dripsy's new hairstyle." Pam paused to think.

"We want *this*," Harriet said, thrusting a picture from a magazine in front of Pam's eyes. Freddy craned his fluffy neck but couldn't see it.

"But that is a style for a wittle girlie doggie, dear." Pam put on her spectacles for a better look. "Dripsy-Wimpsy might feel a wittle silly."

Freddy growled even louder. He was quite sure that if Hideous Harriet was choosing his hairstyle, he would end up looking utterly ridiculous.

"Well, Daddy wants this one and he's the mayor, so just do it!" Harriet ordered. Then she blinked her little piggy eyes and sounded as sweet as honey. "*Please*, of course."

Pam looked doubtful, but she couldn't really

argue; the mayor was the mayor, after all. She twanged on some pink rubber gloves and advanced toward Freddy.

Poor old Freddy, what could he do? He had no choice but to let Pam wet his hair, shampoo him, and put perfume on him. He kept up an incessant growl of threats throughout the whole ordeal. Next she sprayed him with pink liquid that made him cough and splutter. With an electric shaver, she cut away all the hair around his stomach and from the top half of his legs.

After what seemed hours of torture, Pam stood back. She beamed with pride at her work. The twins, who had been pulling faces at Freddy and sniggering throughout, now had tears of laughter dripping down their cheeks.

"One last thing and we're finished. That's a nice necklace for a doggie." Pam smiled when she saw the Moonstone. She hung a little tag next to it that read DRIPSY-WIMPSY, FARFANG CASTLE.

"Yes, we gave it to him for his birthday," Harriet replied, and glared at her brother to make sure he didn't give them away.

Freddy felt sick with dread when at last Pam took off the muzzle.

"My, what a pwetty wittle doggie," she exclaimed.

Freddy ran to the mirror and howled with horror. There in front of him stood the world's most ludicrous-looking poodle. He was bright pink, and Pam's work with the shaver had left him with a pair of woolly shorts, a cropped vest, and little fur socks. There he stood, a descendant of the proudest and fiercest werepack in the history of Wolfenkind. From Sir Rathbone to Flasheart and now to him! This was nothing less than a tragedy.

"I was supposed to be a hero!" he howled.

The twins shrieked with triumph at their greatest joke ever.

"Now who's the pink one, Wimpsy?" Harriet smiled at her glorious revenge. Freddy bared his tiny teeth and turned to face them.

Whoosh!

He threw himself at the Pukesome Twosome in a blur of pink fury. The twins cried out and ran toward the door. Freddy blocked their way, his snarl dripping with spit.

"I hope wittle Dripsy-Wimpsy wikes his new hairstyle?" Pam said hopefully.

"Like it?" Freddy yapped in disbelief. "I absoto-talutely hate it, you silly fruit fart."

Fortunately for Pam, she couldn't understand his woofy words.

Meanwhile, Chariot was trying to sneak toward the door. Freddy spotted him and skidded into his cousin's feet, knocking them from under him. As Chariot fell to the floor, Freddy jumped high and landed with a yelp of delight on his cousin's soft, flabby tummy. Chariot gasped in shock. Freddy jumped up and down as if he were on a trampoline.

"Take that." He landed again.

"And that!" He tried a somersault.

"Get him off me!" the boy wailed, and turned over to crawl away. Freddy jumped onto his back and started pulling Chariot's underpants up from under his trousers with his teeth.

"Ow, help! He's wedgiefying me!"

"A Major Melvin Wedgie," Freddy agreed.

The strain on the material was too great, and it tore away. Freddy fell to the ground, still holding a square of Chariot's underpants in his mouth. He spat it out with fiendish glee. The boy gasped with relief.

"Ha-ha-hardy-ha!" Freddy yelped in triumph.

"Dunderbrain dog," squealed Harriet.

"Oh, dear!" Pam murmured in alarm. "I have never, ever seen such a naughty doggie."

"Oh no? Well, watch this, Pammy-Wammy!" Freddy jumped onto the counter. There lay all Pam's instruments of torture: baskets of rollers, clips, brushes, scissors, bows, tags, shampoos, color sprays, and perfumes.

"Now then, Dwipsy, down you get. Don't make Pammy angwy!" Pam sounded concerned.

"I'll sort him out," Harriet cried, running for a mop she had spotted in the corner of the room. As she ran for it, Freddy, with little barks of delight, started kicking all Pam's baskets onto the floor. They fell with a terrible clatter.

"Take that, Pammy," yelped Freddy. When poor Pam tried to pick him up, Freddy bared his teeth.

"Don't dare touch a werewolf, *human*," he snarled, and sent some of the pink spray and shampoo flying through the air.

Then everything happened at once.

With a jangle of the bell, the door opened. In walked Mrs. Snythe-Bottom in a full-length red fur coat, carrying her blue poodle. As she entered, Harriet swung the mop with all her might.

Wham!

She whacked Freddy on the backside. Freddy and every remaining bottle of pink, blue, and green poodle dye flew through the air. He sailed over Mrs. Snythe-Bottom's head and out through the door, and he landed roughly on the footpath outside with a yelp of pain. The bottles of dye, however, tipped out all over the snooty customer and her poodle. Standing together in dripping pink, blue, and green, they howled with fury. The Putrid Pair squealed like giggling pigs. Poor Pam looked around in despair at her wrecked parlor.

"Do come in, Mrs. Snythe-Bottom," she squeaked miserably. "I am almost weady for wittle Fi-Fi's twim."

Mrs. Snythe-Bottom was not impressed. "You'll pay for this, Pam. That's a promise." The dripping woman pointed at Pam with long red talons.

Before the Putrid Pair could tear their eyes from the terrible scene, Freddy raced away down Main Street as fast as his pretty legs could take him.

CHAPTER EIGHT:
BATTY

Freddy didn't stop running until Pammy's Poodle Parlor was out of sight behind him. Eventually he grew tired and began to trot nervously down Main Street. People who passed him pointed and laughed out loud. He was the daftest-looking dog anybody had ever seen.

"Haven't you ever seen a wolf before? Shake in your shoes!" he barked defiantly.

Nobody screamed, fainted, or ran away to safety. They just continued laughing. *So much for being menacing*, Freddy thought miserably as he passed the butcher shop. He looked up at the rows of dripping meat. He was starving. There was nothing like the thought of food to take Freddy's mind off his disgrace. He hadn't had any breakfast, and it was now eleven o'clock.

He pressed his little wet nose against the window.

"Yelp!" He jumped high into the air in shock.

Somebody had just sniffed his backside!

"Great green vomit!" he woofed, turning round in a fury.

There stood a scruffy, hairy mongrel. Its long black-and-white hair fell down in strands over its big black eyes. If the dog hadn't just sniffed his backside, Freddy would have liked it immediately. It was exactly the kind of dog that he would have wanted as a pet. He almost smiled at the mongrel, but then he remembered the terrible situation he was in. It was bad enough that he was a poodle. If the Fang Council ever found out that he associated with other dogs too, it would only make his crimes worse. So instead, he shooed it away.

"Go home, boy, go on!" he ordered, pointing his ears in the other direction. He was not expecting the dumb animal to understand. The dog bared its teeth.

"I ain't no *boy*!" it replied crossly.

Freddy could hardly believe his ears. It sounded like a woof and a girl's voice at the same time.

"You can *talk*?" he yelped loudly. "I don't believe it. Fantabulous!"

The other dog snarled in annoyance.

"If you can, why shouldn't I, smelly pink poodle? Be cheeky again and I'll bite your tail off. And that's a promise!" With a flick of her long scraggy tail, she trotted away down Main Street.

"No, wait!" Freddy yipped, scampering to keep up with her. "I wasn't cheeky." He didn't want the dog to run away; it was so exciting being able to talk to her.

"I just thought dogs like you were too stupid to talk," he gasped breathlessly. The mongrel stopped abruptly and growled at him. Freddy looked at her sharp teeth and realized his mistake.

"I mean, I thought I could only talk to wolves."

Now the mongrel stared at him in disbelief. She flicked her hair out of her eyes with a toss of her head.

"Wolves?" She narrowed her eyes and inspected Freddy. "Wolves can't talk. They're just wild animals, ain't they? And anyway, what kind of dog would want to talk to one of *them*? Even if you tried, a wolf would finish off a smelly little puke like you in one bite. Before you even opened your big trap."

"Little puke?" Freddy was outraged. "Well, that's where you're wrong, actually. Because I *am* a wolf! Not just some common *dog* who sniffs backsides." He stuck out his chest and paraded in front of her. "I am one hundred percent wolf!"

The hairy mongrel looked at him as if his brain were mashed potato, and then howled with laughter. Freddy caught his reflection in a shop window and sagged miserably. How could anyone believe he was a wolf underneath this curly pink disguise?

"You are a silly, pink, smelly little poodle, and I don't like poodles," the dog told him slowly and clearly. "You are also a liar, and I don't like liars, *and* you don't have no manners." She flicked her tail. "So clear off out of my patch."

"No manners?" Was a common mongrel really telling a Lupin how to behave? Freddy puffed up in outrage. He was descended from one of the oldest, noblest of werepacks.

"At least I don't sniff backsides," he yipped.

"That's what I said, ain't it? No manners. Didn't your mother teach you nothing when you was a puppy? You always do the Hello Sniffing dance when you meet someone."

"No way!" Freddy yipped, his ears drooping in dismay. How revolting! This was certainly not part of a werewolf's rituals. He had no intention of performing that dance. The mongrel looked at him with disgust and trotted away once again. Freddy tried to keep up.

"Clear off, stink-pup!" she called back.

"No, wait. It's because I'm . . ." Freddy looked around desperately. Next to him was a travel agent's with a revolving globe in the window.

"I'm from Australia," he shouted, always willing to lie at a moment's notice. The mongrel stopped, her curiosity getting the better of her.

"Where's Australia?" she wanted to know.

"On the other side of the world."

The mongrel looked doubtful. To her "the world" meant Milford.

"Near the pooing field?" she asked. (She meant, of course, the public park.)

"No, far away on the other side of the ocean, where everybody is upside down."

The mongrel started to rumble, thinking he was being cheeky again. Freddy thought desperately.

"Look here." He ran to the shop window and pointed at the globe with his ear.

"See?" he barked. "That ball is the world. We, I mean *you*, live on the top, but I come from under there, *down under*. Australia."

The dog looked at the globe suspiciously.

"Is that why you talk funny?" she yipped at last. "You don't sound like no proper dog."

"Yes." Freddy laughed with relief. "That's right, cobber. G'day mate, everybody loves good neighbors. And that's why I don't do Hello Sniffing. In Australia dogs shake paws like this." He held out his paw. "That means good manners there."

"So what are you doing here, then?"

"I was dognapped because I'm so valuable. But thanks to my ingenious plan, I managed to escape. I was just running away from them now—the baddies, I mean. They tried to disguise me by dyeing me pink and putting perfume on me!"

"So that's why you smell so bad?" She nodded, trying to work out if she believed him.

Freddy might have been insulted if it hadn't been for the fact that he smelled bad to himself.

The mongrel narrowed her eyes.

"If you're lying, I *will* bite your tail off," she promised.

"Cross my heart I'm telling the truth. I never lie," Freddy lied.

He held out his paw. After a moment the dog gave a small woofy laugh and held out her own paw.

"What's your name, then, stink-pup?" she asked.

"Freddy," he yipped. "What's yours?"

"Batty. Did you live on the Wildside in Australia?"

"What's the Wildside?" Freddy asked.

Batty raised her hairy eyebrow. This dog was a stranger for sure—he didn't know anything!

"The Wildside is where I live. Running around on your own, looking after yourself. I don't need no human." She flicked her head proudly.

Just then there was the sound of sirens approaching Main Street.

"Shush!" Batty whispered, her ears standing high and searching for the noise. "Police! Humans! We have to hide, quick." She began to run at full speed down the road. Freddy tried his best to keep up with her.

"But why are we running away? We haven't done anything wrong."

"Wise up, stink-pup, we're on the Wildside. That's against the humans' law. They always try, but they can't never catch me!"

Batty disappeared down a narrow alley. Freddy followed, wondering what on earth his new friend was in trouble for. And then he realized. They were outlaws! Oh *yes*, he liked the sound of that. He was already feeling more like a hero again.

CHAPTER NINE:
OPERATION SAUSAGES

Freddy had been taught to believe that he was naturally superior to dogs. It was a well-known fact that in comparison to any wolf, a dog was by far the stupider. Now that they were an outlaw band, Freddy would be happy to give Batty the benefit of his greater intelligence.

"In there, quick." Batty pointed at a garden shed with her ear.

The two dogs streaked inside the open door and waited as the sound of the police sirens grew louder and louder. Freddy became a little less brave and a little more alarmed as the noise became deafening. Of course, it's easy to say you want to be an outlaw—until the police actually start chasing you. He sighed with relief when the sound faded and, at last, disappeared.

"They've gone!" laughed Batty, flopping onto the floor.

"But why are they chasing you?"

"'Cause I steal sausages from the red meat shop," Batty replied proudly. "I'm the best sausage thief in Milford."

"Oh, that's brilliant!" Freddy cried, very impressed. "Of course, *I* was the best sausage thief in the whole of Australia, you know. And that's twenty million times the size of Milford." He licked his paws modestly, as if this were a minor achievement.

Batty looked at him, unconvinced.

"What, you?" she scoffed. "Don't you care that it's against the law?"

"Of course not." Freddy shrugged. "I'm not scared of the police, am I?"

"You seemed to be just now, all right. I never knew a poodle what wasn't scared of the police. I ain't never heard of no poodle sausage thief, neither."

"Well, I'm not an ordinary poodle, am I?" Freddy yipped. The mention of sausages had made Freddy's stomach grumble. He hadn't eaten since before the High Howling the previous night. "I love sausages. I can eat twelve in one go. I'd do anything for sausages."

"Oh yeah? So what's your plan for breaking into the red meat shop then, stink-pup?" Batty laughed.

"I don't have one . . . yet," he admitted.

"Hungry?" Batty asked sympathetically.

He nodded miserably.

"Didn't your dognapper feed you?"

Freddy shook his head even more miserably.

"Well, let's go and break some rules, then," she laughed. "Or are you too much of a poodle?"

Freddy's ears perked up.

"No. I'm not scared of anything!" he yipped, but then he began to get a teensy bit worried. "But . . . we won't get caught, will we?"

"Don't worry, Stinky, we ain't going to get caught." Despite his great stories, this pup would never survive on his own on the Wildside, Batty thought. "You'd better stick with me."

The eyes and muzzles of the two dogs peeped out from behind a tree opposite the butcher shop. Freddy's mouth watered at the sight of all those strings of sausages hanging in the shop window, but the door was closed.

"How do we get in?" he asked Batty. There was a door handle that looked impossible to open with his doggie paws.

"Easy," she told him with a pitying smile. This silly poodle didn't have a clue. The sausage thieves were obviously not very bright in Australia if he was the best of the bunch. "It's getting out again what requires the skill." She lay down behind the tree with her chin on her paws.

"What are we waiting for?"

"Shush," she instructed.

Freddy huffed and thought he might sulk. He was a wolf, after all! He should not be bossed around by a mongrel dog, even a brave and pretty one. Batty didn't notice his sulking; she was too busy watching all the humans walking down Main Street. Her ears jumped when she saw what she wanted.

"Get up, Stinky," she whispered. "Here's our way in." She pointed her nose at a mother walking with her son and daughter and pushing a pram toward the butcher's.

"Operation Sausages is a go!" she woofed

dramatically. "I'll go into the shop and you wait outside and keep guard. The mom will take ages trying to get her puppy's carriage through the door. That gives me time to run in and out—I'll be quicker than a tail's wag. When I grab the sausages, run as fast as you can and we'll meet back at the shed."

Freddy nodded. Batty's tail was swishing with excitement.

"First we have to be nice to the puppies. That's how we get in." The mongrel ran over to meet the family. Freddy followed eagerly.

As soon as she reached the children, Batty started scampering to and fro in front of them. She woofed charmingly, flapped her ears up and down, and tossed her pretty hair from side to side. It had the desired effect.

"Here boy, sweet doggie," cried the little girl, letting go of her mother's coat. Batty ran to meet her and allowed the girl to pat her on the head. Batty licked her face.

"Urg," the girl giggled.

"Not too close!" her mother warned.

"Come on, Stinky," Batty woofed. "Make them like you. It's easy."

The baby gurgled with delight at Batty's funny antics. As Freddy trotted up to the children, he recognized the boy from his class at school. Daryl Spanner. Freddy didn't like him one bit. Daryl Spanner took one look at his classmate and laughed out loud.

"What a stupid dog," he taunted. "She looks like pink cotton candy."

"She's so sweet," cried the little girl. "A little Barbie doggie."

It was all more than Freddy could bear.

"I'm not a *she*, I'm a *he*. In fact, I'm a *wolf*!" he yapped. "Who asked you anyway, Spanner? And tell your snotty sister that I'm not sweet and I'm not Barbie. I'm *fierce*!" He bared his teeth and woofed menacingly at the children. The little girl screamed.

"Shhh, you big baby, I'm trying to be your friend," Freddy barked urgently. The girl screamed even louder.

"Keep away, you smelly hound," the mother yelled, and whacked Freddy on the head with a rolled-up umbrella.

"Youch!"

"Stupid poodle," Daryl Spanner said as his

mother dragged them away down the street. She had forgotten all about her visit to the butcher shop. The family disappeared and the shop door remained firmly shut.

"It didn't hurt me!" Freddy lied, woofing after the mother. "So there!" *They won't say I'm sweet again,* he thought, very pleased with himself. He imagined Sir Rathbone would have behaved in a similar way. He felt his father would have been proud of him. For the first time since his Transwolfation, Freddy felt he had lived up to the reputation of a menacing werewolf at last.

He turned to face Batty, who snarled at him in total disgust.

"What?" Freddy woofed. It suddenly occurred to him that Operation Sausages had not gone according to plan.

"It wasn't me!" he said, trying to look innocent. Batty was not impressed. He tried to look sweet. Batty was still not impressed. He tried to look tough. Batty snorted.

"You silly pink stink-pup," she growled. "All you had to do was make the puppies like you. They always like me."

"They said I was a girl, and Spanner said I looked like cotton candy," he yipped in outrage.

"What's cotton candy?" Batty asked.

"It's fluffy and pink and it looks like . . . *me*." Freddy sulked. That made Batty laugh; she was never able to stay angry for long.

"But how do you know what they was saying?" she asked, returning to her lookout spot behind the tree.

"Oh derrr! I am *English*, aren't I?" he scoffed, following her.

"No. I thought you was Australian." She looked at him closely.

"Same thing, mate," he replied nervously. The trouble with telling lies is it's so difficult to remember them all the time.

Batty was looking at him in a very strange way. Then something occurred to Freddy.

"Don't you understand what humans say?"

"Of course not!" yelped Batty. "No dog can."

"Well, I can," Freddy barked pompously, showing off again. "Perhaps because I am no mere poodle. Perhaps because I really am a wolf."

"Since when can wolves understand humans either? Even pink ones," Batty laughed. However, she looked at Freddy with new respect. He may be stupid, pink, smelly, spoiled, and convinced he was a wolf, but being able to understand humans was an impressive skill.

"Woof-tastic!" She smiled, bashing Freddy with her paw. He felt very proud to have impressed so clever a dog.

"Don't you know *any* words?" he asked her.

Batty had to think hard. It was so long since she'd had a human to look after her and talk to her that she couldn't really remember.

"I know my name, 'Batty,'" she said at last. "And 'walk' and 'dinner.' And one other horrible word . . . '*Coldfax*,'" she whispered with a shudder. "It's a word every dog knows and fears."

"Coldfax? What's that?" Freddy asked.

"It's a terrible place, over the dark hill. It's where they take dogs from the Wildside. No free dog knows what it's like inside Coldfax, 'cause no dog ever comes back out. There's no escape. At night you can hear the dogs howling, but you don't never see them." Batty shook herself and they were quiet for a while.

"I'm sorry I ruined everything. I always do, although I never mean to," Freddy said mournfully, looking over at the butcher shop. Batty looked at the smelly poodle with pity.

"Oh well, pick your ears up, Stinky," she urged, pushing him with her paw. "Operation Sausages isn't over yet. Look." There was a man walking toward the shop.

"You stay here, Freddy. Plan B is too dangerous for you."

Freddy didn't like to appear cowardly, but he had already made a mess of things once. Batty would probably be safer without him. He watched her go with a nervous wag of his tail.

"Be careful," he yipped. "I'll come if you need me!"

Freddy watched as his new friend walked close behind the man. He heard a little bell tinkle as the man entered the shop, completely unaware that Batty was following him. Freddy's heart was beating fast as the man turned to close the door.

That's when Freddy saw his face. He had thin white cheeks and huge, staring eyes behind thick, round spectacles. It was a face that every were-pup had been taught to fear. Freddy gasped in terror. There, leading Batty into the store, was Dr. Foxwell Cripp, werewolf hunter—the man who had shot his father with a silver bullet.

CHAPTER TEN:
DR. FOXWELL CRIPP

Dr. Foxwell Cripp had only one mission in life, and that was to destroy all werewolves. When he was a young boy, he had once spied over a neighbor's fence and seen what so few people have: the Transwolfation of a man into a wolf. He had hidden in fright as the wolf he had known only as Mr. Patterfall—a gentle, kindly old man—paced slowly around his garden in the moonlight. Cripp had seen no terrible violence, no attacks made by the wolf, but that one vision had been enough to spark his curiosity . . . and his loathing. The old man died soon after, before young Foxwell could work up the courage to confront him about his secret. Instead, Cripp watched horror films, read ghost stories, and believed all the tales about were-wolves' savagery. Everything he saw convinced him more that werewolves were terrible and fearsome creatures. He was certain that only he, who knew that they truly existed, could save the world from their evil.

He had spent his life piecing together little bits of stories and scraps of evidence. He did hours of research in libraries. He tracked down rumors of strange happenings behind high walls and in ancient forests. His most valuable piece of evidence, which he found in the dusty attics of a half-ruined castle, was a confession. It had been extracted three hundred years earlier from a man arrested for theft. In an effort to save his own life, he had promised to tell the "greatest secret known to man," and so he had betrayed the werefolk. He had told of the Grand Growling, of the High Howling, of the Hidden Moonlight Gathering, of the Fangen and the Weren. He had told how a Fangen's first Transwolfation takes place one hundred and twenty-five full moons after his or her birth. He had told of *The Red Book of Wolfen Names*, which was always entrusted to the Grand Growler.

This book contains the names and human identities of all the werefolk in Britain. Worse than all this, the man had revealed the power of the Moonstone and how it might be harnessed to find the wolves. He had been judged insane by his captors and left to die in the dungeons. His confession had lain forgotten until Dr. Cripp found it and realized that he now had the key to completing his mission. He must find the Grand Growler.

The Hidden Moonlight Gathering of Werefolk was held only twice a year, unless there was a blue moon due, which was not very often. Whenever there was, however, an extra meeting was called to elect the Grand Growler. It was far too dangerous for the werefolk to meet more often. The gatherings were held at Farfang Castle or else at the home of another member of the Fang Council. But it is not easy to hide the evidence of a Blood Red Hunt. And slowly, over many years, Dr. Cripp pieced together his evidence. Farmers sometimes told tales of livestock going missing. Mysterious beasts were often spotted against the light of the full moon. Strange growling and howling was heard on the night air. These occurrences were often reported in the newspapers as "big cats" escaped from zoos, but Cripp knew better. He made it his business to find out about all such rumors, and he very carefully marked an *X* on his map when he did.

The Lupin family had been very careful that no such rumors should ever exist in Milford. It was the one area on Cripp's map of Britain that had had no *X* anywhere nearby. For twenty years, despite all his efforts, he had never found another wolf, for the werefolk knew about him. They, too, watched and had their spies. And they had always outwitted him . . . until one infamous night some six years ago.

Cripp would never have thought of going near Milford until he received a note written in blood.

You will find the Black Wolf of Milford in the stone circle, on the full moon.

At last, Cripp thought, he would finally have proof that there were more wolves—that his neighbor had not been the only one. Milford was famous for its ancient stone circle. It lay in a clearing in the woods nearly two miles from Farfang. There, Cripp had waited and the wolf had come—running out of the dark forest into the moonlight. That wolf had been Flasheart Lupin. Cripp had shot the wolf and believed that thanks to him, one town, at least, had been freed from the terror of the beast.

But now all his trails had run dry. He had not discovered the Grand Growler, and his map had been no help to him. So after many years he had returned at last to Milford, the only town in which he knew for certain a wolf had once lived. Perhaps there were more? Little did he know that a wolf was watching him, then and there, right on Main Street.

Freddy jumped back behind the tree. If Dr. Cripp saw him, he would shoot him with a silver bullet for sure. His skinny pink legs shivered with fright.

"Why is he in Milford?" Freddy whimpered. "I must warn Uncle Hotspur."

A terrible thought occurred to him. What if Dr. Cripp had been to Farfang Castle already? Did he know the Lupin family's secret? It didn't matter how much Freddy disliked his uncle, he would have to warn him. As Grand Growler, Uncle

Hotspur was guardian of the Wolfen Names. If Dr. Cripp found those, no Weren or Fangen would be safe again.

And what about poor Batty? She was a dog and not a wolf, so he hoped Dr. Cripp would not harm her. Though that is like hoping a shark in a swimming pool with your best friend won't eat him because sharks usually hunt seals. Not much comfort, really.

He could see the ghastly figure of Dr. Cripp, but there was no sign of the mongrel. Shivers of fear went down his spine. He caught a glimpse of himself in the window's reflection and almost laughed. As if anyone would suspect *him* of being a werewolf. His disguise was perfect. He crept nearer until he could peek through the glass door. There was Batty lying quietly on the floor behind the dreaded man.

Freddy watched them carefully. He was determined to come to the rescue if he was needed, Dr. Cripp or no Dr. Cripp.

Inside the shop the butcher was carefully weighing out some pork chops.

"Will they do, sir?" he called over his shoulder.

"Fine, thank you," Dr. Cripp replied. Batty lay silently behind him, trying to appear invisible. Neither of the men had noticed her. The butcher began to wrap up the chops, and Dr. Cripp cleared his throat.

"I wonder," he began with a small cough. The butcher waited expectantly.

"I wonder if you ever have large orders for red meat on a night with a full moon?"

"A full moon?" repeated the butcher, perplexed.

"Yes indeed," Dr. Cripp went on. "Last night, for instance, was a full moon. I wonder whether there was a feast held anywhere in Milford. I hear rumors that there was. A High Howling of were—" He paused, licked his lips, and began again. "A feast for people who like to eat red meat. Meat dripping, quite dripping, with blood!"

Dr. Cripp gave the butcher what he imagined to be a charming smile.

"I haven't heard of no feast in Milford," the butcher said sternly.

"Are you quite sure? No extra orders for kidneys, or steaks, or tender baby lamb?" the doctor hinted.

"Well, now that I think of it," said the butcher,

"the mayor had a little party for his nephew up at the castle last night, but I wouldn't call that a feast."

"What's that?" Dr. Cripp's eyes lit up eagerly.

"Well, it was young Freddy's tenth birthday. Funny, though, the party was a month late. My Susan has the same birthday, and she was ten last month."

"Why, that makes it his one hundred and twenty-fifth birthday for a wolf! On the night of the full moon!" squealed the doctor in delight. "Of course! How marvelous. It must be the High Howling."

The butcher narrowed his eyes.

"*High What-do-yer-say?* It was a birthday party, I've told you." He scowled.

Dr. Cripp ignored him. "With lots of meat, though. You did say that, didn't you?" he asked eagerly, his glasses steaming up.

"Well, I suppose you could say so. Two hundred steaks and five dozen lambs' hearts," the butcher admitted reluctantly.

"Oh, sweet words, it must be true," he whispered to himself. "Who else but the werefolk need so much blood red meat?"

"What's that you say?" the butcher demanded suspiciously.

"Oh, nothing, nothing." The doctor tried to remain calm. "How much for my chops?" He paid, then turned and put his hand on the door handle. He paused very casually to ask one more question.

Batty was now alert. She watched his hand as it slowly started to turn the handle. It was her plan to grab the sausages from the window display as he opened the door, then flee at top speed.

"And what was the name of the castle where the party was held?" He smiled repulsively.

"Farfang, of course, where Mayor Lupin lives. Everybody knows that." The butcher had had enough of his strange customer.

Batty watched as Dr. Cripp began to open the door. Suddenly he laughed out loud and let go of the handle.

"Lupin, Lupine, of course! Don't you see? It means 'like a wolf.' I've found him, I've found the Grand Growler!" He cackled madly, then screamed in surprise as a wild beast jumped for his throat. Or so he thought.

It was Batty, flying past him. She had already begun to jump when he had let go of the handle, and she now found herself stranded in the middle of the window display. She grabbed some sausages and turned to face the butcher. She was trapped with no hope of escape.

"Is that your dog?" the red-faced butcher bellowed at Dr. Cripp.

"Certainly not! I cannot stand the smelly beasts," Dr. Cripp replied.

The butcher glared at Batty. "This is the last time you steal from my shop, you miserable, hairy hound." He turned round and reached for his huge meat cleaver.

Ding-dong!

The bell rang as the shop door opened. There on the outside handle hung Freddy, pulling down for all he was worth with both tiny paws. With his whole weight he had just managed to swing the door open.

"Not another one!" roared the butcher, racing around the counter with his sharp cleaver.

"Run, Freddy," Batty called, and leaped toward the door. As Dr. Cripp tried to close it with his foot, Freddy fought to keep it open.

"Stop those dogs," ordered the butcher.

"With pleasure," laughed Dr. Cripp. Suddenly he took a tiny silver gun from his pocket. He aimed it carefully at Batty as she tried to pull the door wide, but Freddy was too quick for him.

"Youch!" cried the hunter as the poodle's sharp little teeth sank into his ankle. Cripp dropped his gun and cradled his leg.

The dogs ran for their lives down Main Street, the string of sausages sailing behind them like the tail of a kite.

"Miserable mongrels," the furious butcher yelled after them. "You were no use either, you great cream cake," he informed Dr. Cripp.

"I am maimed . . . ," the doctor began, but his words died as he stared intently at a ring on his finger. It was silver with a tiny white stone set in the center—a Moonstone. This was Dr. Cripp's great weapon in the hunt for werefolk, and the stone was now hot, so hot that it was burning his finger. It could mean only one thing: a werewolf was close by.

"But it cannot be," the doctor said to himself. "They were only dogs. No werewolf can go abroad unless the full moon is in the night sky."

He looked down at his ring once more. He remembered the glorious night when he had fought the Black Wolf of Milford. The stone had burned his hand that night. One of those dogs must be a werewolf.

"I wonder," Dr. Cripp said, his eyes narrowing. He stood up, and with a somewhat unsteady step began to follow in the direction of the two dogs, a crazed gleam in his eyes.

CHAPTER ELEVEN:
CAPTURED AGAIN

"I can't do it," Freddy called back into the shed.

"You have to balance on three legs," Batty told him in amazement. How could a dog be so pampered he doesn't know how to pee?

"Oh, I get it now." Freddy laughed with relief—he had been holding it in for hours. When he had finished, he returned to the shed.

Full after their meal of stolen sausages, the two dogs curled up against each other and slept for a while. Freddy drifted into an uneasy dream, where he was running back to Farfang, chased by Dr. Cripp. But when he arrived, it was too late to save the werefolk from the dreaded man. He jumped awake with a start. Batty raised a sleepy ear off her eye to look at him.

"What's the matter, Stinky?" she said sleepily.

"I have to go home to Farfang Castle right now!" he told her urgently. "I've already wasted too much time."

"Is that in Australia?" Batty yawned kindly. She felt sorry for Freddy being so far from home.

"Grr . . . ," Freddy rumbled uncertainly, not sure what to say. He had almost forgotten his elaborate lies from earlier. In fact, he couldn't remember exactly what he had said to Batty. This was always a great danger for him, losing track of the lies he told.

"How will you get there?" Batty continued. "Is it far to the other side of the world?"

"Grr . . . ," Freddy replied again, at a loss for a good story. "Yes . . . Farfang Castle is in the woods on the other side of the river," he said at last. He was hoping that Batty's doggy brain wouldn't work out that he had fibbed.

"What does 'castle' mean?" Batty growled, her eyes narrowing.

"It's a huge house built of stone, with towers and a big gate," Freddy snorted. "Fancy not knowing that." He was a rather foolish dog to try to make fun of her just then. Batty, however, wasn't foolish in the least, and she didn't like being lied to.

"I know the place you mean. It's the House of Howls, where the Red Wolf lives," she snarled suspiciously, standing up.

"How do you know about the wolf?" Freddy gasped with horror. It was supposed to be a secret. If everybody in Milford knew, they would never be safe again.

"Every dog around here knows about him. None of us can stand wolves—horrible, vicious animals. You said you was from Australia. The House of Howls is on the other side of Milford, not the other side of the world." Batty was starting to get angry now, and Freddy began to feel nervous.

"No dog would never go near the House of Howls. The Red Wolf don't even sound like a normal animal, more like some sort of . . . I don't even know what. It's a terrifying place."

"Well, yes, Uncle Hotspur can be quite scary," Freddy admitted, then grimaced at his own stupidity.

"*Uncle?*" snarled Batty. "The Red Wolf is your uncle? How is that possible?"

"Grr . . . ?" he answered.

"What about Australia, then?" she snarled louder.

"Grr . . . mmmhmnn?" Freddy's mind was a blank.

"You've been telling me lies all the time," she growled at last.

"It wasn't me!" Freddy yipped idiotically, backing toward the door.

"Well, who was it, then? Who are you, anyway? I told you, smelly little poodle, that if you were lying I'd bite your tail off." Freddy didn't want his tail bitten off. He turned, ran through the door, and scooted off back down the alley. Behind him he heard the sound of pursuing paws. He had only one thought in his head, to run, run, and then run some more. He ran out of the alley, into the street, and straight into a large net.

"What *now*?" he yipped in confusion. His paws were caught up in the net, and the more he struggled, the more entangled he became. Was it a trap laid by Dr. Cripp? He saw two men standing back and laughing. One was the butcher and the other held a second net.

Dr. Cripp was not there, but Freddy had

been captured again, and this time he was very frightened.

Just then he heard some familiar, welcome woofs.

"Don't worry, Freddy, I'm coming, I'll save you," called Batty. She hurled herself onto the net and started to tear at it with her teeth. The men tried to approach her, but she barked at them fiercely.

"Run, Batty, or they'll catch you, too. It's the butcher," Freddy yipped in warning.

"You never left me in the red meat shop, did you, Stinky?" She tore away at the net again.

"Look out," woofed Freddy, but it was too late. The other net was flung on top of the brave mongrel. She gave a howl of fury that any wolf would have been proud of, but she was well and truly trapped.

The men hauled up the nets and threw the two dogs into the back of a small van. It smelled of fear. A thick wire mesh separated the dogs from the front seats. The doors were slammed shut, and the net man climbed into the driver's seat. The butcher stuck his head through the window and smiled with satisfaction.

"It's them sausage thieves, all right." He nodded.

"You couldn't mistake that ridiculous pink one."

"Well, it's Coldfax Fort for these two now," said the driver with a significant nod of his head.

The butcher's eyes lit up with delight. "So I won't be seeing them again anytime soon?"

"Not ever!" the net man said icily, and with another laugh he drove away.

At the mention of Coldfax, Batty's eyes had widened with terror. She understood very well what was going to happen. The blood drained from Freddy's head and his tail went limp.

"I'm so sorry," he moaned with shame. For almost the first time in his life, he really meant it: He meant he was sorry for somebody else and not himself.

"So am I, little stink-pup." Batty licked his head through the netting. "If I hadn't frightened you, this wouldn't have happened."

"I'm sorry I lied," he whispered.

"Well, I suppose you did try to tell me you were a wolf." She shook her head in confusion. "Is it really true?"

Freddy nodded.

"Well, I'll have to try and believe you, then."

With that, the two frightened friends huddled

against each other. The van bumped along through the growing dark toward the dreaded Coldfax Fort. Freddy struggled under the weight of the net but managed to balance on his hind legs long enough to look out the rear window. The slim figure of Dr. Cripp slid out from the shadows. He had overheard the butcher and the net man and knew exactly where his werewolf was heading. The werewolf hunter gave a ghastly smile and nodded to him. Freddy was certain that his enemy was going to track him down, and he was powerless to escape.

CHAPTER TWELVE:
COLDFAX FORT

The two dogs shivered miserably as the van lurched and rattled toward Coldfax Fort. Batty had feared that terrible name since she was a pup. Freddy tried to comfort her with brave words, but she only whimpered in reply. All too soon the van slowed to a stop.

"Two more prisoners," the driver cried, flinging open the doors.

Freddy and Batty, still entangled in the nets, struggled to stand. They could hardly see after being in the dark van. But they could still smell, and that was bad enough. They were surrounded by the scents of sad and miserable dogs. There were no happy scents at all, but there was plenty of fear.

"Oh, Stinky," Batty woofed in dismay, "this is awful."

"Don't worry." He nudged her. "We're getting out of here, I promise."

"But no dog has ever escaped from Coldfax," she yipped.

"But I'm not a dog, I'm a wolf, remember? And what's more, I am . . . the Plan Master," he woofed, all pompous once more. "And nobody can ever keep me locked up," he barked defiantly at the driver. He had conveniently forgotten the events of the past sixteen hours.

For all her worries, Batty had to laugh. He really was a very silly pink dog and clearly *not* a Plan Master.

"Bark all you like, pathetic poodle," the driver chuckled nastily. "Nobody'll hear you, nobody'll save you."

He pulled the dogs out of the van. They yelped as they landed on the hard floor and rolled out of the nets. They were in the middle of a square cobbled courtyard. Tall walls rose on three sides, with many tiny windows staring down. Behind them was a high, spiked iron fence with a stone archway. The arch was barred with a metal portcullis, such as you might see in an old castle. The net man handed them over to another man and then drove his van away. The portcullis began to lower.

"Run, quick," Batty yelped, her ears flat against her head as she tore away.

But before she could escape, her head was caught neatly in a loop of rope hanging from a long pole.

"Oh, no, you don't," the other man said, sounding more bored than cruel.

He slipped leads around their necks roughly, then jerked them through a small door and into a dark room. The door was slammed behind them.

"I'm not scared, you know," Freddy barked at the door. The only sound was the man's footsteps echoing off the stone walls.

Freddy looked around. The room was small, with a stone floor and a tiny window too high up for them to see anything.

"Where are all the dogs?" Batty wondered. She could smell them but not see them.

"Don't know," Freddy replied. "Perhaps there aren't any after all. . . ."

"Hhhhhooooowwwwlllll." A terrifyingly loud and mournful howl came from beneath them.

The two dogs looked at each other in dismay.

"What was that?" Batty whimpered.

The unearthly howl came again. Freddy couldn't make out any words in the noise. It just sounded like sorrow, terrible sorrow.

"It's the creepiest howl I've ever heard," he admitted in a whisper. "And I've heard Uncle Hotspur."

As the howl came once more, Batty's ears stood high in alarm.

"I don't never want to meet *that* dog," she said decisively. "It don't sound natural."

"Nor me," Freddy agreed. "But I'm not scared!" he added in a hurry.

"Why not? I am," Batty whispered. Freddy was about to say something pompous about wolves once again, but he was stopped by another shivering howl.

"I'm not scared of any dog in the world," he woofed loudly and defiantly. It didn't sound convincing.

"OH NO? You will be when I get to you!" came a huge roar outside the door. It wasn't the sorrowful voice of the howler, but a new, savage, and mean one.

The door flew open with a crash, and the dogs yelped with fright.

"Stand still for inspection, dregs!" slavered the brutal bark. Batty and Freddy backed away in alarm. There in the doorway stood a huge gray wolfhound. He was almost the size of Sir Hotspur when he was a wolf. He bared his teeth and glared with hatred at the two prisoners. Freddy, mesmerized with fear, was only just able to raise his eyes to see the human who stood next to the beast. He could have woofed with surprise to see a tiny old lady with a perfect bun of white hair. She wore small half-moon spectacles, a brown sweater, and a sensible checked skirt. She might have been anybody's teacher or granny.

"Cerberus, what a terrible din. Do pipe down, I can hardly think." She tugged sharply at the wolfhound's ear. His barking became a steady growl, and he continued to glare at Freddy.

"Now then," said the woman, bending down to inspect the bewildered dogs. "I don't like the look of these two," she told Cerberus. "Especially this pink one. Looks like a real sneak, a sissy if ever I saw one."

"I do not!" Freddy yipped despite his fear.

"Keep quiet when the Commander speaks, dreg!" Cerberus ordered viciously.

"Is he giving cheek, Cerberus? Keep your eye on that one. He looks slier than any dog I ever saw." The old woman looked over the top of her glasses at Freddy with distaste. She gave a shudder. She absolutely loathed all dogs except Cerberus. It made her ideal for her job as Commander of Coldfax Fort. She was only too glad to make sure her dogs were never seen on the streets again.

"Well, girls, I have only three rules: no barking, no running, and no breaking any other rules I think of."

"Girls? Are you blind? I'm not a girl!" Freddy barked loudly. He simply never knew when to keep quiet.

"Freddy, shush," warned Batty.

Too late. Cerberus sprang forward and knocked Freddy onto his back. Freddy yelped with terror as the beast snarled in his face, his teeth dripping.

"No barking in Coldfax, nose-drip. No laughing,

no talking, no running, no howling, no *nothing*, unless I tell you. Is that understood?"

"Yes," Freddy whimpered.

"'Yes, sir!'" Cerberus snarled.

"Yes, *sir*," Freddy replied shakily. The wolf-hound gave a final snarl and took his paws off the poodle's heaving chest. The Commander laughed.

"Well done, boy. You show the sneaky little beast who's boss." She patted him on the head.

"Move it faster, nose-drips. You make me sick," Cerberus added helpfully as the Commander took their leads and pulled them out the door.

"I don't think he likes us," Freddy whispered to Batty.

Coldfax Fort was shaped like a giant letter *H*. A corridor ran the full length of one of the long "legs" of the *H*, with cells on either side. At one end was the main entrance and the Commander's office, and at the far end was a heavy oak door that led down to the dungeon. The Commander led the two dogs down this corridor and past a long row of empty cells. Each had a barred iron door and straw scattered over the floor. Batty could tell by the smell that this was where the dogs lived, but where were they? The Commander pointed at a cell.

"This'll be your home for the rest of your miserable lives," she laughed, prodding Freddy with her foot.

"The only way out of Coldfax alive is to be adopted. And nobody ever adopts a dog from here. Because you are the biters, the pooers, the scratchers, the farters, the thieves, and the filthy mongrels. Nobody wants you. You'll be here till your pink curls are gray, and so will your scruffy friend." She gave another nasty laugh.

Cerberus didn't know what her words meant, but he knew that when the Commander laughed, his prisoners would be miserable. That made him laugh too—a rough, terrible, mean laugh.

"You'll never leave here. I'll always be watching you now," he snarled.

"Wait a minute, what's this?" The Commander yanked at the little tag that Pam had put on Freddy's collar.

"Dripsy-Wimpsy? Well, the name is spot-on. Farfang Castle? So you're not a stray after all." She sighed. How she hated the idea of a dog having a safe, warm home.

"Let's take them to the Pit for Walk Time. I'll decide what to do about the pink one later."

Freddy and Batty looked at each other with grim determination. They both knew what the other was thinking. Somehow, some way, they *must* escape from Coldfax Fort.

"Down there, dregs," Cerberus snarled.

They had reached a narrow passageway on their left that ran off the main corridor. A door in the middle of this corridor opened onto several steps, which led down into another courtyard. Like the entry courtyard, this one was surrounded on three sides by the building and on the fourth by a high fence topped with barbed wire. This was the Pit. It was filled with more than a hundred dogs of every shape and size, pacing slowly in a circle. The man who had thrown Freddy and Batty into the cell sat on a chair in the middle, watching. He was still bored, but not as much as the dogs. A sadder sight Freddy had never seen. There was no yapping, nor sniffing, nor fighting, nor chasing—just a slow and sorry walk.

"Go on, then. Walk! Walk!" the Commander ordered, removing the dogs' leads.

Batty and Freddy walked grimly down the stairs and into the stream of dejected dogs. Not one pair of eyes rose to greet them. There was no Hello Sniffing dance. The dogs just silently stepped around them and carried on their walk to nowhere.

The newcomers joined the slow circle. The Commander and her dreadful hound disappeared, and the door slammed shut with an echo. Freddy seized the opportunity.

"Okay," he whispered, "the Plan Master has already worked it out. We build a tunnel, bring out the earth in our pockets, and drop it on the ground during Walk Time. The enemy'll never know." Freddy had watched too many old war films.

Batty wrinkled her nose. What was he barking on about? What were *pockets*? She had other things on her mind.

Batty was on full alert. Her pretty ears were standing tall and her tail was held high. All the usual rules of Doggery didn't seem to apply here. The Hello Sniffing dance isn't just polite, but essential to know who is friend and who is foe—who will play and who wants to fight. Batty caught whiffs of anger and danger. But from which dogs she couldn't tell. She needed every sense ready to spot trouble. And Freddy, she had little doubt, would be no use whatsoever if it did come. Wolf or not, she would have to take care of him. He wouldn't stand a chance without her.

Freddy, of course, saw himself in a quite different and far more heroic light. Even as a poodle, he felt the blood of Sir Rathbone in his veins. He was the Plan Master and was going to take care of Batty. She wouldn't stand a chance without him. But most urgent, he must escape from Coldfax and warn his werepack that Cripp was in town. They were in the gravest danger.

"Now, you always need a passport to escape," he yapped excitedly. "Which dogs are good at forgery?"

Batty wasn't listening. From behind her she could hear a low rumble. It sounded like danger. She looked back nervously.

"They don't say much, do they?" Freddy yipped, looking around. "It's a well-known fact that dogs are stupid. Except *you*, of course. That's probably why they haven't escaped. I would have by now."

Batty heard the growls from behind her again.

"They look a bit cowardly," Freddy whispered far too loudly. "Probably too scared to run away."

"Will you put a paw in it? Unless you can say something helpful," she growled at Freddy.

"I'm planning our escape. What's more helpful than that?" he snapped.

The growling behind them was steadily growing. Batty looked around with much concern. She was trying not to listen to Freddy, but unfortunately, bits of his nonsense kept reaching her ears.

"I could climb down the wall on a rope made of blankets. Or . . . or . . . how about . . . hide inside a wooden horse? That's what some famous old guys did once. I won't give up like these no-hope hounds."

"Don't you ever shut up?" Batty growled in despair.

The bored man stood up from his chair in the center of the courtyard. With a stretch and a yawn he walked through the slow parade of dogs. He climbed the few steps, unlocked the door, and left the Pit.

The dogs came to an immediate halt. As one they raised their drooping noses and turned to look at the newcomers. Batty and Freddy moved closer together. There was not a snuffle or a sniff. The tension was unbearable. Freddy couldn't bear anything that was unbearable.

"Boo!" he yelped. Every dog jumped, including Batty. She glared at him in disbelief. How was she ever to keep such a silly creature safe? All the surrounding dogs began to growl quietly. Suddenly a large boxer jumped out and snarled at Freddy, who leaped back in alarm.

"Who's the coward now, poodle?" He looked at the smaller dog with disgust and sniffed him.

"You don't smell like no proper dog. Don't look like one neither, not a real dog, that is. What are you really, pink poodle?"

"A wolf, can't you tell?" Freddy yipped defiantly.

"We don't like poodles in here." The boxer gave an unpleasant snarl.

The other dogs growled in agreement.

"They don't never live on the Wildside. You wimps always need a human; you're always snitching to them."

"No one calls my friend a snitch," Batty snarled, moving in front of Freddy.

"Yeah!" Freddy yipped. "So if you do it again, I'll tell her."

The boxer looked down at Batty and snorted.

"Like I'm so scared of a *girl*," he laughed sarcastically. He and Batty glared at each other.

"Bruno! Is that any way to talk to a lassie? You should be scared of girls. They'll cause you more trouble than anything else in the world." This new bark came from a small white-haired terrier, who limped up to the boxer. The big dog immediately drooped his ears.

"You'll have no luck with the ladies that way, laddie," the terrier continued, and gave a woofy chuckle. The boxer's nose went red with embarrassment, and he stuck out his lower jaw in a sulk.

The terrier laughed. "Well now, who do we have here?" He and Batty danced the Hello Sniffing, and he introduced himself as Hamish.

Freddy sat down quickly and held out his paw.

"He's a stranger. He don't understand no good Doggery," Batty woofed.

"He's strange, all right," the boxer yipped.

"He doesn't understand when to keep his

muzzle closed." The terrier looked at Freddy and shook his head.

"That's 'cause he's a poodle," the boxer growled. "Don't never trust 'em."

"My hairy ears! Bruno, you talk nearly as much rubbish as this wee pink lad. I've told you many times; don't judge a dog by its breed."

The boxer stuck out his lower jaw grumpily once more.

"Bruno is in here because of a poodle, you see; she led the dogcatcher to his hideaway." Hamish turned to Freddy. "You're a brainless buffoon, lad," he laughed. "But we'll give you one more chance. Good Doggery is more important here than anywhere. There is no escape from one another and no escape from Coldfax."

"Yes, we know," Batty sighed sorrowfully.

"Speak for yourself!" Freddy barked. "I'm going to escape even if you can't. Just 'cause you're all afraid doesn't mean I am."

The terrier was unimpressed and gave the pink poodle a scornful laugh.

"Big words for such a silly dog," Hamish yipped. "Wait till you've been here for ten years." (He meant dog years, of course.) "I've seen nobler hounds than you sink under the dread of Coldfax. There is no escape. Hiding, climbing, digging, running, jumping. Many dogs have tried, but not one has succeeded. I received this for my third attempt, when Cerberus caught me." He held up his lame paw.

Freddy and Batty gasped with sympathy. The other dogs whined gently.

"Don't dare insult those who have tried and failed. You have not been tested." The surrounding dogs growled their agreement.

Freddy, crestfallen indeed, now spoke up with great remorse. "I'm sorry, I didn't mean to be rude. It's just that I need to escape. My pack is in great danger," he woofed miserably, thinking of Dr. Cripp and *The Red Book of Wolfen Names*.

"All the dogs here have a family they care for. Do you think yourself so special, so Crufts?" Hamish replied sternly, though this time with some softening of his tone.

"Erm . . . I don't know," Freddy said in confusion. He had no idea what "Crufts" was.

They heard footsteps outside.

"*Walk*, quick, everyone!" the terrier woofed quietly. The circle of dogs began to pace again. Hamish turned toward Batty and Freddy. "Remember, there are two rules. Do nothing to anger Cerberus; he is as savage as a man and without mercy. And no more talk of escape; it is dangerous for us all."

With that, the dogs returned to the endless circle. Batty and Freddy joined in without another word.

CHAPTER THIRTEEN:
CELLMATES

After Walk Time Batty and Freddy found themselves in a cell with three other dogs. Hamish, Bruno, and a King Charles spaniel.

"Just my luck!" the boxer woofed roughly, and glared at them in disgust.

"Why, too scared to share with a wolf?" Freddy yipped defiantly.

"Oh, joy," the spaniel yawned lazily. He was sprawled out on the straw licking his paws. "I always hoped to meet a miniature pink wolf." He snorted through his damp nose.

"Och, leave the wee pup alone. It's not his fault he looks like a ridiculous sissy. Who did this to you, son?" Hamish asked with a friendly woof.

"The Putrid Pair . . . two *human* pups. They dognapped me," Freddy told them with a snarl. "And when I get out of here, I'll . . . I'll . . . I'll *show* them."

"Careful, laddie, watch your talk," the terrier woofed with a significant frown. He pointed his ears at the spaniel.

"This is St. John." (He pronounced it Sin-john.) Batty waved her ears and turned a few circles in welcome. The spaniel totally ignored her.

"He was once the Supreme Champion at Crufts," Hamish added.

Batty raised her eyebrows in surprise. St. John smiled as if he were the king of the world rather than a prisoner in Coldfax.

"What's 'Crufts'?" Freddy asked, wholly unimpressed.

St. John nearly choked with disbelief. Hamish laughed.

"Where have you been all your life, lad? Crufts is the most famous dog show on the planet. And the Lord St. John here was once the Champion. The best dog in the world, *apparently*."

St. John looked away from them all coolly.

"Says who?" Freddy frowned. Hamish, Batty,

and Bruno all seemed more impressive dogs to him, in their different ways.

"Says humans what want dogs to wear perfume like them," Bruno snarled at Freddy, clearly smelling his terrible stench. "You'd probably win too. No real dog would ever be in a *show*."

Freddy glared at him, and so did St. John.

"We still don't know your names, though," Hamish went on.

"I'm Batty and this little pup is Freddy," she told them. "We're here for stealing sausages."

"You will excuse me if I don't rise for petty criminals," St. John sniffed.

"I'm the best sausage thief in Milford," Batty informed him with an angry swish of her tail.

"Oh dear, how un-Crufts you are." The spaniel gave a wheezy laugh and turned his back on them. "Now, if you please, I need my beauty sleep."

"Just ignore the Supreme Champion—that's what we do," Hamish told her with a woof. "So, a sausage expert, hey? A lassie after my own heart."

"Did you steal sausages too?" Batty gasped in admiration.

"Only more than any other dog in history," he yipped proudly. "But that was years ago. You would have been only a pup." He sighed. "It's a long while since I ate a sausage."

"You will again once we bust out of here," the boxer woofed, then slapped his paw over his mouth.

"Put a paw in it, lad," the terrier yipped in warning, giving a meaningful wag of his tail toward St. John.

"So you *are* planning an escape?" Freddy yipped loudly. "Me too! I'm going to break out tonight."

Batty put her paw on his muzzle to shut him up.

"My hairy ears!" the terrier growled. "It's bad enough trying to keep Bruno quiet."

"I'm sorry about this silly pink pup. But you'll like him when you know him better," she promised.

"I won't," Bruno growled.

Hamish looked unconvinced too. "Maybe," he said. He dropped his growl very low. "But no more talk of escape. It's not safe." He pointed his ear toward the sleeping spaniel.

"Why?" Freddy whispered back. "Doesn't he want to leave Coldfax?"

"Shush!" Hamish growled. The dogs drew closer together.

"St. John was Supreme Champion at Crufts, but . . ."

All the dogs paused and looked over at the now-snoring spaniel.

". . . but when he went to collect his ribbon . . . *disaster*," Hamish continued.

"What happened?" Freddy yipped.

"St. John lost control in his excitement and did a poo on the judge's shoe," the terrier told them solemnly. "He lost his title."

"A *poo*?" Freddy exclaimed. "Fantabulous!"

The other dogs looked at him in surprise.

"How can you cheer at a fellow dog's disgrace?" Hamish frowned.

"Freddy, will you try to be more like a dog?" Batty whispered crossly in his ear. Freddy sighed. Surely he should be allowed to laugh at such a silly story.

"It was on the television, of course, so every dog in Britain knew," Hamish carried on. "His owner put him in here in disgrace. St. John even *wants* to stay because he knows he can't show his muzzle in public again."

"It's him what tells Cerberus about anyone's escape plans. He's always listening," Bruno muttered in disgust.

"He's a *spy*?" Freddy yipped. He knew what it was like living with spies around. Harriet and Chariot were forever telling tales about him to Uncle Hotspur.

"But why does he want to stop *us* from escaping?" Batty was puzzled.

"If he tells tales he gets treats as a reward," Bruno told her.

"So no more loose words, for Cerberus always finds out. Now get some sleep," Hamish ordered. "You've had a big day."

Freddy and Batty curled up together. Freddy looked around the cell miserably while the other dogs drifted off to sleep and began to snore. The floor was made of heavy flagstones that no dog could dig through. The tiny window was too high to reach. The heavy iron bars of the door were too narrow for even Hamish to pass through. There was no chance of escape. Unless . . .

Freddy looked at the door. The cells were

designed for dogs, not boys. Between the top of the door and the ceiling was a gap of about twelve inches. It was too high for a dog to reach, but maybe a skinny boy could climb up the iron bars and squeeze out over the top. The Plan Master began to smile. It was against all the rules of the Hidden Moonlight Gathering ever to reveal your true identity to a human, but no one had ever mentioned anything about telling a *dog*, had they?

Freddy noticed the other dogs' snores growing deeper and decided it was safe to wake Batty with a friendly nip on the ear.

"What now, Stinky?"

"I have a plan, but first I need to tell you everything about me. You must promise to believe me, and you're not allowed to bite my tail off."

Batty gave a little growl but nodded her ears in agreement.

He told her the whole truth about himself, his family, werefolk, *The Red Book of Wolfen Names*, and the dreadful Dr. Cripp. Batty's ears perked higher and higher with astonishment as she listened. It had been hard enough to believe that Freddy was a wolf; now she had to believe that he could be a boy, too? She began to growl suspiciously again. But somehow it made sense. She sniffed him once more. He had never smelled right, never smelled like a dog. That was when she believed him.

"You smell like a human!" she woofed in realization. "That's why you stink. I thought it was because you had that pukey perfume on, but you really do smell that bad underneath!"

"Oh, great, thanks!" Freddy almost sulked but was too pleased to have convinced her.

"I must get out and warn Uncle Hotspur," he said urgently.

"But why do you care about your family when they are so horrible to you?" Batty asked. She had never had anyone to care for her.

"They're more than my *family*; they're my *werepack*, the pack of Sir Rathbone. It's my duty to help them, or any werefolk in danger, even if I can't stand them. It's the Pact of the Fangen. Cripp may be on his way to Farfang already. He mustn't find the Grand Growler."

"Well . . . even if poodles can be boys . . . or *wolves* . . . I'm still not sure that it'll work," Batty growled.

"Yeah, it will, listen. . . ."

Freddy's plan was quite simple. Somehow he would remove the Moonstone, turn back into a boy, and climb over the gap at the top of the iron door.

"Then I'll find the keys and let us all out!" he woofed excitedly.

"Shush . . . What's a *key*?"

"It's a little metal stick that humans use to open doors," Freddy told her pompously. Batty was impressed by Freddy's knowledge, but she, of course, was more used to planning maneuvers than he was. She immediately pointed out several problems with his plan.

"How do we get the wolf-stone off you? Where will you find the metal stick that opens the door? And what about Cerberus?" She pointed her ear out into the corridor, where they could hear wolfhound claws on the stone as he patrolled.

"I haven't thought of those bits yet," Freddy admitted, suddenly feeling less optimistic.

Batty inspected his chain collar for a moment.

"I see the stone but don't know how to break the chain," she growled. "I'll have to think about it."

"But I have to escape now!" Freddy yipped. "Dr. Cripp is dangerous."

"And so is Cerberus, and you can't get past him even if you got out of the cell! Don't worry, Stinky." Batty bit his ear affectionately. "I'll think of a way of turning you into a boy again, but we can't do it tonight. We need to find a tool or some way of breaking that chain. The best thing we can do now is sleep and save our strength."

With that, the two dogs snuggled down and slept.

St. John licked his paws and yawned. *Oh dear.* He smiled to himself. *How Crufts. A human, a wolf, and a pink dog all in one? Just wait till I tell Cerberus.*

Freddy was wrong about Dr. Cripp. He was not on his way to Farfang Castle. He was hiding in the woods as night approached, looking up at the walls of Coldfax Fort. On his finger the Moonstone shone brightly.

"I've got him now!" he cried loudly. He had found another werewolf at last.

Suddenly the same deathly howl that Freddy and Batty had heard earlier echoed from the heart of Coldfax once again. Dr. Cripp stopped his cackling and froze.

In their cell two dogs jumped to their feet in fright.

"What on earth *is* that?" Freddy woofed.

"Oh, that's just the ghost hound of Coldfax," Hamish replied sleepily. "Nothing to worry your pretty pink head about. Nighty-night, then."

CHAPTER FOURTEEN

A VISITOR

The following morning, a few miles away, Sir Hotspur was raging over his breakfast.

"Blast that foolster Frederick!" he bellowed. "He's ruined everything and now he's disappeared. I've searched the whole castle. He's a disgrace—a disgrace, sir! When I find him, I'll chop him into twenty pieces, make him into a pie, and throw it into the sewer. That I will, sir!" His eyes were wild under his bushy red eyebrows. He thumped the table, and all the plates jumped up and landed with a crash.

Chariot's piggy eyes opened a little wider. Harriet, however, just smiled as she poured milk on her cereal.

"I saw him five minutes ago, Daddy." She smiled sweetly at her father.

125

"What's that?" He turned his bloodshot eyes to her. "Where?"

"I wanted to fetch you, but he tried to bite me."

"The *animal*!" Sir Hotspur roared. "And are you hurt, my precious angel?"

"No, I'm not scared of a *poodle*!" she scoffed.

"Ha! Quite so, madam, quite so." He slammed his fist down again.

"I saved her, Dad," Chariot butted in, not wanting to be left out.

"No, you didn't." Harriet kicked him under the table.

"Yes, I did." He kicked her back.

"So where is the foolster?" fumed Sir Hotspur.

"He was on his way to the lavatory," Harriet said with her nose in the air, giving her brother such a hard kick that he had to hold his breath.

"The *lavatory*? But I've looked everywhere!" Sir Hotspur spluttered.

"Not *inside* the castle, Daddy," she corrected. "He's a *dog*, so of course he wanted to poo on your lawn, just like his friend did last week."

"*Poo?*" Sir Hotspur could barely speak the word. "On my *lawn*?"

This was dangerous ground. The only thing

Sir Hotspur loved more than himself and Sir Rathbone was his lawn.

"But he's not a dog *now*, Harry. He'll have transformed back. He'll be that menace Frederick again." The thought gave him some relief.

Chariot looked alarmed. Harriet had nearly given away their trick with the Moonstone. If their father realized that they knew he had a Moonstone, they would be in for it. Worse still, if he knew they had taken it . . .

Harriet, however, was calm.

"I know he's a boy, silly Daddy." She smiled slyly. "But he said he'd do it on your lawn anyway."

News of such despicable behavior was more than Sir Hotspur could take. He trembled with outrage and turned a dark shade of purple.

"To think this *creature* has polluted the glory of Sir Hotspur! I . . . I . . . mean Sir *Rathbone*, of course." His cheeks wobbling with temper, he stormed downstairs and outside into the garden.

Sir Hotspur was relieved not to find the dreaded poo on his lawn after all. He charged back into the castle to search once more for his troublesome nephew. As he walked along the corridor that led from the Great Hall to the Tower, he noticed that his study door was open. With a grim smile he walked in, certain of finding the foolster at last. There was something wrong. Things had been moved on his desk. The keys to his drawer were not exactly as he had left them. Even the heart of Sir Hotspur could beat a little too quickly at the idea that his secret may have been discovered. He opened the drawer and then sat down on his chair in fright. The Moonstone was gone!

"Where is that foolster?" he cried louder than ever.

There was one man who thought he knew the answer to that question. Later that afternoon a man walked up to the gates of Coldfax Fort. He looked around nervously as if he didn't want be seen, knocked on the door, and was shown inside.

Freddy and Batty had not slept well. Freddy in particular had been very unnerved by the howling of the ghost hound. He had spent most of the night with his paws clamped over his ears. He hated ghosts even more than he hated spiders.

"And is it really a ghost?" he asked the next morning, feeling very tired and sorry for himself.

"Some say so." Hamish nodded. "Though none have seen it. Whatever it is, it prowls the dungeon underneath us."

"It's a headless hound from hell," Bruno growled in a low voice. "Sent here for all eternity for the greatest crime ever known."

Freddy's tail drooped. Batty's hairy eyebrows rose higher. "What's that?" she rasped.

"Don't know," The boxer admitted. "But they say he has no mercy."

Everyone looked at one another. It was too creepy.

"If he's headless, how does he howl?" Batty wondered.

"Good question, lassie," Hamish laughed. "But don't fret. Whatever it is, as long as you stay up here, you'll be fine."

There was no breakfast served in Coldfax, and by the time the miserably bad lunch was served, Freddy's stomach was howling. Straight after lunch, the dogs were sent down to the Pit for Walk Time. While they were there, the door opened and the Commander appeared with Cerberus.

"Fetch the pink one," the old lady told the guard dog. "He has a visitor." It was uncanny how the huge wolfhound seemed to understand the old lady's words. Freddy understood them only too clearly.

"Batty, he's coming for me!" he yelped.

The two dogs watched in fright as the slavering hound ran toward them.

"Freddy, what have you done *now*?" Batty yipped. The poodle seemed to get in trouble no matter what she did to help him.

"I have a visitor," he cried. "What if it's Cripp? No one else knows I'm here."

Cerberus ran quickly. The other dogs parted nervously around him.

"Come with me, pink stench," he snarled.

"Why?" Freddy whimpered.

"No questions, nose-drip!" Cerberus roared.

"Please, may I come too?" Batty woofed.

"Step back in line!" the great beast snarled at her.

Freddy had no choice but to go with Cerberus. Batty watched as the little pink poodle hopped up the stairs. The Commander opened the door without a word, and, with a frightened backward glance, Freddy left the Pit. Cerberus, however, stayed to watch over the other dogs.

"Poor little Freddy," Batty whimpered.

"Come on, lassie," Hamish whispered as he walked past. "It won't help if you make Cerberus mad. Walk Time now, walk, walk!"

Reluctantly, Batty started to walk. Her nose pointed sadly at the ground in front of her, just like the miserable dogs around her. As they walked with their heads down, nobody noticed St. John walk slyly up to Cerberus. He began to whisper in the wolfhound's ear. Cerberus listened, then shook his head and snarled at the spaniel. St. John had to work hard to convince the guard dog that what he was saying was true.

"You can tell from his smell," he woofed at last.

As it had made sense to Batty, so it did to Cerberus now. He gave a nasty laugh, nodded, and left the Pit. The door closed behind him as he bounded down the corridor after Freddy.

With trembling legs, Freddy followed the Commander down the stone corridor toward her office.

"Heel, heel, won't you? Keep up," the old lady snapped as they walked.

Freddy had no wish to heel. He didn't want to meet Cripp but was powerless to escape him. At last the Commander reached the door and opened it, shoving the reluctant poodle inside with her foot.

Freddy jumped with surprise and relief. Before him stood not Dr. Cripp but Uncle Hotspur, the very wolf he needed to talk to.

"Here is Dripsy-Wimpsy," the Commander said as they entered. "When I saw his tag I knew I should call you."

Sir Hotspur had received the Commander's call just after he discovered that the Moonstone had been taken. He had raced over to Coldfax Fort as quickly as he could. When he saw Freddy, he almost exploded.

"Pink, sir? *Pink?* What is the meaning of it?" he huffed with purple cheeks. "You, sir, are a foolster!"

"He's certainly a most absurd creature," the Commander agreed.

"He is a disgrace, madam!" Sir Hotspur interrupted. "A disgrace."

Freddy looked down at his clawed toes in sorrow. For a moment he had almost forgotten how ridiculous he looked.

"I want a word with my nephew alone, madam, if you would be so kind." Sir Hotspur smiled.

"Your *nephew*? Sir Hotspur?" The old lady turned in amazement.

"Just a pet name, madam. No relation, really. No!" The mayor shuddered at the thought.

"As if such a great man could be related to such a ridiculous little dog," the old lady laughed.

Sir Hotspur puffed his cheeks at the flattery.

"Quite so, madam! The boy, er, *dog* is a foolster." As soon as the Commander left the room, Freddy ran forward and began to jump up around his uncle's knees.

"Dr. Cripp is in Milford," he yipped loudly.

Sir Hotspur, of course, understood none of this, but he did spot the Moonstone around his nephew's neck. He grasped the chain and lifted him into the air.

"What is the meaning of this, sir? How could you plan such infamy? To actually wish to remain a poodle! Who helped you? You could not fasten this chain yourself. How could any

Lupin wish to be a *dog*? Impossible. Let me think. . . ."

Sir Hotspur did think. He looked at his nephew's ridiculous pink fur cut into vest, shorts, and socks. No boy would ever do this to himself, he was sure. Besides, Freddy was too stupid to find the Moonstone.

"*Harriet*, of course." He gave a chuckle of pride at his daughter's genius.

Freddy's furious yaps confirmed his suspicion.

"My clever girl." Sir Hotspur smiled. "More clever than she knows. Now, let me see that chain," he said, ignoring the barks and changing his grip on Freddy so the unfortunate dog was left dangling by his hind legs. Lupin gave the chain a pull, then he dropped the furious poodle back on the floor.

"That'll hold, sir! It would take my fangs to break that chain. No hound here could do it." Uncle Hotspur's voice dropped to a nasty growl. "You'll stay here, sir, until the Great Pack has forgotten you ever existed. Until the stain upon Sir Rathbone's memory has faded, and until I am Grand Growler once more!" He gave a cold laugh.

"You're not leaving me in this place?" Freddy howled with horror at the dreadful news.

Sir Hotspur only laughed once more.

"But Cripp's here! It's not funny. It's . . . it's . . . scarifyingly . . . totally . . . gggrrrrr!" He couldn't make his uncle understand. The whole of the Hidden Moonlight Gathering was in grave peril. All Sir Hotspur could hear, of course, was a series of noisy barks and yips. The Commander returned with tea and buns.

"What a hideous noise," she wailed. "I'm afraid I don't like this dog much, Mayor."

"Never could stand a dog, madam," he replied. "Poodles are the worst of the lot. As for a pink one? *Disgraceful.*"

"But you have to listen to me!" Freddy woofed in vain.

"So you aren't taking Dripsy-Wimpsy back to Farfang, then?" the Commander asked joyfully.

"No, madam. He'll be staying here for a long time," Sir Hotspur replied with a nasty gleam in his eye.

"I know exactly what you mean, Mayor." The Commander gave a knowing look.

"Quite so. And how is the other matter?" he

asked with a glance at Freddy, who continued to bark madly at him.

"Oh, everything is under control!" She gave a cruel smile. "And this ugly little beast isn't going anywhere either."

Poor old Freddy wailed in fury and frustration at his plight. Not only had Sir Hotspur betrayed him, but he was blind to the danger the werefolk were in. There was only one thing for it: Somehow Freddy must stop Cripp himself. And whether he was a wolf, a poodle, or a boy, that was exactly what he was determined to do. Freddy Lupin had one hundred percent hero's blood in his veins, and he meant to use it.

CHAPTER FIFTEEN:
ESCAPE PLANS

Batty was overjoyed to see Freddy return safely to the cell. He breathlessly told her about his meeting with Uncle Hotspur, while she tried her best to comfort and calm him. Sometime later the bored man came to fetch St. John, who gave a superior smirk as he was led from the cell.

"Where are they off to?" Freddy yipped noisily.

"Outside Walk Time," Hamish replied. "Now, we must be quick. Here's the escape plan. . . ."

"Escape?" Batty whispered. "But I thought you said there was no way out?"

"So far as St. John knows, that's true," Hamish laughed.

"Escape? Fantabulous!" Freddy yapped at top volume.

"Shush." The other dogs cringed.

"Do you always have to be so thoughtless, lad?" Hamish hissed.

Freddy had a think. "Not *always*," he decided.

"Good." Hamish smiled. "Or else we couldn't tell you our plan."

"Our escape plan!" Bruno woofed, even louder than Freddy had.

"My hairy ears!" Hamish yapped in exasperation. "You two have the brains of a human." This is, of course, a terrible insult.

"Well, yes, I am very clever." Freddy was pleased to have had his genius recognized.

"Stop showing off, Freddy," Batty growled.

"I'm not, I'm just saying . . ."

"Yes, you was showing off," Bruno agreed.

"The next dog to make a *woof* won't be going on any escape!" Hamish yipped in frustration, louder than anyone else had.

The other dogs looked at their paws, feeling like naughty puppies.

"Can we have some quiet?" the terrier whispered. "Now listen . . ."

Freddy was tempted to point out that now, by his own rules, Hamish was not allowed to escape, for he had woofed first. For once, however, he kept quiet.

The dogs gathered closer.

"I wasn't sure whether to tell you at first. I saw the wee pink lad here, and no offense, Freddy, lad, but you didn't look tough enough—"

"And we knew he'd snitch," Bruno interrupted.

"Well, I'm not too worried about *that*, as Cerberus clearly can't stand you. He's always been very tough on silly dogs," Hamish continued. "However, you did prove yourself to be a fool. But *you*, on the other paw, lassie, are a sausage stealer—the smartest, cheekiest, and quickest profession on the Wildside. So I just have to give you the chance. And, of course, Freddy's in our cell so he has to come along too, despite everything."

Batty was not a show-off, but she couldn't help but look proud and pretty at this news. Her tail wagged beautifully.

"Not tough enough?" Freddy sulked at the appalling insults. "A *fool*?"

"Are you ready for the plan?" Hamish yipped.

Batty nodded, and Freddy, despite a temptation to sulk, found that his curiosity got the better of him. Bruno walked over to the straw where he and Hamish slept. He pushed it away with his paw.

"There you go!" Hamish yipped proudly.

There in the flagstone floor was a metal grate. Freddy and Batty looked at each other.

"Go on, lad," Hamish woofed.

Bruno pushed his paw down with all his strength on one corner of the grate, and the opposite end popped up. Hamish clamped it with his tiny teeth, and he and Bruno tugged the grate away, leaving a hole about twelve inches square.

"A tunnel!" Freddy and Batty woofed together.

"Aye, well, it's a drain, actually," Hamish corrected them.

Batty put her muzzle down the hole and sniffed, then jumped back in excitement.

"Outside! I can smell the Wildside," she barked.

"Oh, aye," Hamish agreed. "There's a way out, all right, we just have to find it. It's like a maze down there."

"Whenever St. John is gone, one of us has a look around," Bruno told them.

"But what about the ghost hound?" Freddy suddenly remembered.

"You just hope you don't meet him," Bruno growled, sounding very brave.

Batty looked at him with new admiration, and the boxer went red.

"But what if the ghost hound comes?" Freddy gasped.

"Well, he only seems to howl at night, and we don't go down then," Hammish replied. "But these are only the drains. The entrance to the dungeon is through that door there." He pointed with his ear to a heavy wooden door at the end of the corridor. The sight of it made Freddy's blood go cold. He shivered.

"Now that you two can help, we'll find the exit in no time," Hamish added cheerfully.

Freddy's face fell at the thought of going down into the dark, where the headless hound haunted. He was more scared of ghosts than anything.

"I'll go right now!" Batty volunteered without hesitation.

But she never had a chance, for suddenly there was a loud commotion in the corridor. Quickly the dogs pushed back the grate and the straw. Yaps began to echo along from cell to cell.

"A human is here!"

"To adopt us!"

"Someone to take us home!"

It was unbelievably good news. Never in the history of Coldfax had a human wanted to adopt one of the inmates.

"This is our chance, Batty!" Freddy said in excitement. "If we can be adopted, that means we'll be *outside*."

Batty raised her eyes at him affectionately, secretly sorry for the poor little smelly poodle. Surely no self-respecting human would want *him* as a pet. "Stinky, if you are chosen, you must take your chance and go. Don't worry about me," she reassured him.

Freddy was instantly dismayed. It hadn't occurred to him that he might have to leave Batty behind. "I'm so sorry, but I must save my pack. As soon as I'm a boy again, I'll come back and adopt you."

Batty whacked him reassuringly with her tail. He was going to need all the help she could give him. "Sit up on your back legs," she instructed.

"Then offer to shake paws." Freddy did as he was told.

"Should I look fierce?" he wondered.

"Don't be silly, Stinky," Batty laughed. Freddy's ears drooped. "You have to look *clever*," she added.

That idea cheered him up immediately. The dogs lined up.

Bruno looked strong, Hamish clever, Batty charming, and Freddy . . . well, he looked pink and silly. What were the chances of *him* being chosen?

The person was coming.

"That one *bites*, this one *smells*, that one *limps*," the Commander said from outside the next cell. The old lady was clearly not going to help one of the inmates go to a happy home. Several dogs couldn't bear the wait and erupted into hysterical woofs.

"Oh, take me!"

"Pick me! I'm sweet! I'm good!"

"Steady, pups!" Hamish instructed. "No human wants a sissy for a dog. No offense, Freddy, lad."

"I'm not a *sissy*!" Freddy hissed in fury.

Bruno sniggered.

Freddy stood up on his hind legs and started a special twirl.

There was the sound of applause. He had obviously impressed the person with his tricks. He jumped around in triumph, then fell back onto the straw with horror.

There, clapping at his performance, stood his greatest enemy.

"Cripp!" he woofed.

Batty, too, had recognized the wolf hunter. She jumped next to Freddy protectively. "I won't let him take you," she growled fiercely.

The Commander looked on in disgust.

"These are the very *worst* dogs—the dregs. You can't really want one of these?" she asked in disbelief.

The ghastly man raised his arm and pointed at the two friends, steaming up his thick glasses in his excitement.

"Yes!" he cried. "Yes, I want one of those two. . . ."

On his pointing finger, the Moonstone shone brightly in its ring. Fortunately, Freddy's own Moonstone was hidden by the little silver tag Pam had put on him.

Much faster than I can tell you, Freddy realized the truth. He knew that a Moonstone in the hands of a human was a fearsome weapon. At that very moment Dr. Cripp's blood would be burning hot. The hateful man had discovered Flasheart, and now he had discovered Freddy. Who would be next? Before he remembered that being brave might also be dangerous, Freddy flew through the air and caught Dr. Cripp's finger in his sharp little teeth. The doctor let out a high-pitched shriek.

"The pink one has bitten me," he wailed. "Again!"

Cerberus flung himself against the iron bars in a spitting rage. "Let go or die, you putrid pink dreg," he snarled savagely.

"Freddy, be careful," Batty woofed with concern. Her silly friend could be brave at the most dangerous moments.

"Oh no, laddie. That's no way to be adopted," Hamish groaned.

Freddy dangled in the air, holding on to the ring with all his might.

Crash!

The hunter fell backward onto the stone floor

of the corridor and Freddy onto the straw in the cell. The ring had fallen off into Freddy's mouth, and, with no other place to hide it, he swallowed it with a gulp.

"Well done, Freddy!" Batty cried.

Freddy turned to see Cerberus's red-rimmed eyes glaring with hatred at him, a deep, terrifying growl coming from his throat. Freddy almost preferred the idea of going with Dr. Cripp to staying here with the wolfhound.

"You ought to keep these vicious monsters caged," the wolf hunter gasped. "That ring was vital to my work. *Vital*."

"Oh, it'll come out the other end quite soon, don't you worry," the Commander replied.

"Well, you must notify me the instant it does," Dr. Cripp said angrily.

"So you won't be wanting the poodle after all?" The old lady smiled in relief.

"The *pink* one?" The doctor snorted through his nose. "Of course not! The only thing I want from that creature is my ring back, which revolting job I leave to you, madam. No, it's *that* hairy hound I want." He raised his finger and pointed it again, at *Batty*. Freddy woofed with shock.

"Perhaps she doesn't look like a wolf, but she can't hide from me." The ghastly man giggled madly.

"Batty, don't let him take you! He thinks you're a Fangen," Freddy yapped, horrified.

The Commander reluctantly opened the iron-barred door. Batty ran to and fro, trying to keep away from her.

"Help her, quick. He's going to kill her, not adopt her. It's a trick!" Freddy called to the others.

Bruno immediately jumped in front of Batty. Cerberus leaped at him with a snarl and knocked him against the wall. Bruno fell down, stunned. Freddy and Hamish snapped at the fearsome guard dog's haunches. He turned on them with a snarl and swiped both dogs away easily with his heavy paws, then backed Batty into a corner. In a second she had been muzzled and was yanked on a lead out of the cell. Before any of her friends could reach her, the iron cage door was slammed shut once more.

The Commander handed Batty over to the hunter. Cripp looked at Batty, who snarled at him defiantly, and then with a laugh he pulled her away down the corridor. He smiled in satisfaction.

Only a silver bullet could kill these evil beasts, but he was prepared; he had a silver pistol with him always.

Freddy howled with anguish at the dognapping of his brave friend. As his sorrow echoed around the corridor, it was joined by the eerie howl of the ghost hound of Coldfax.

"He's been missing for two days!" Mrs. Mutton was standing in the kitchen and raging at Sir Hotspur.

"The boy is here somewhere, madam," he lied. "He is a skulking coward. Probably hiding under a bed. Am I to blame for that?"

"You are to blame for frightening him so much he ran away. Do you want to feel the wooden spoon again, Hotspur?" She held up the dreaded weapon.

"No . . ." Sir Hotspur looked more like a naughty puppy than the fiercest wolf in Britain. Nobody knew how old Mrs. Mutton was, but she had looked exactly the same when Hotspur was a boy. Both he and his brother had felt the wooden spoon on many occasions. She was the only creature on the planet he was still scared of.

"Then find him now and bring him home safely," she ordered.

Sir Hotspur glared at her from under his eyebrows and muttered to himself.

Mrs. Mutton raised the wooden spoon again and Sir Hotspur gave a jump.

"All right, madam! But the foolster is a disgrace, I tell you!" Nonetheless, he went out to pretend to look for his irritating nephew.

"Silly old windbag." Mrs. Mutton shook her head as he left the room.

"And don't think I can't see you two," she cried, turning to the smirking pink faces peeping in through the window.

The twins only laughed and ran away. Their father had pretended to be furious with them when he had returned from Coldfax Fort. But they had seen that secretly he was pleased. They had all three made a pact never to tell. The existence of the Moonstone and Freddy's imprisonment in Coldfax were to be a secret among Sir Hotspur and his children. No one would ever know.

* * *

Freddy was inconsolable. Batty was in mortal danger and it was his fault. If she had never met him, she would still be safe now, happily stealing sausages and running away from the police. Freddy had tried his best to help her, but that had not been good enough. Sir Rathbone would never have left a friend in peril. And Freddy would help her now if he could, if only he weren't stuck inside this stupid cell. . . . But of course!

He jumped up, his ears high and alert.

"The drain, quick!" he yipped excitedly.

Hamish and Bruno looked up with questioning ears.

"I'll go through the tunnel and rescue her!"

"But we haven't found the way out yet, lad," Hamish said gently.

"But I have to escape *now*!" Freddy yapped at full volume.

"Hush, hush, lad!" Hamish urged. "You don't want everyone to hear."

"To hear *what*, I wonder?"

St. John's sly voice behind them made the dogs jump. With him were the Commander, the bored guard, and the snarling Cerberus.

151

"Time to pay, pink stench," the wolfhound slavered.

"Only one place to punish *biters*," the Commander laughed. "*You* won't be causing any more trouble in Coldfax."

Freddy started to feel extremely worried.

Just then the mournful howl of the ghost hound once again filled the cell with its eerie music.

"The ghost hound is going to eat you alive," Cerberus laughed horribly.

Hamish's and Bruno's ears fell.

"Take him to the dungeon," the Commander ordered icily.

Freddy gasped with horror. He was being sent to the ghost hound's lair?

"No. Please, I'm sorry, I'll be a good dog, I promise," he whimpered.

The bored man opened the door and the wolfhound charged in. He bowled Freddy over and stood with his heavy front paws on the poodle's chest.

Freddy was just as frightened for Batty as for himself. How could he rescue her if he was in the dungeon? The horror of what awaited fell upon him. Before he could worry any more, he found himself dangling in the air, held in the bored guard's fist. Freddy could hardly breathe, but he managed one last croak.

"Bruno, save her."

"Keep brave, laddie!" Hamish called.

Freddy couldn't answer. The cell door slammed shut. As he was carried down the corridor, the dogs stood silently by the bars of their cells to watch. They had heard what the terrible punishment was to be.

Freddy's terror increased as they drew nearer to the heavy oak door at the end of the corridor. The Commander stepped forward, put a large key into the lock, and turned the heavy handle. With a hideous screech the door swung toward her. Slippery stone steps led down into the pitch black. Freddy smelled cold, dank, stale air . . . and also something much more frightening.

"Take him down," the Commander said.

Freddy whimpered and with his scratchy little toes tried to kick the bored man, but still they descended into the dark. Cerberus paced behind, with a rare and nasty smile. At the bottom was another thick wooden door closed with an iron bolt. The bored man opened it and threw the poodle roughly onto the stone floor beyond. In an instant Freddy scrambled round and charged at full pelt back toward the door, where he was met by Cerberus's bared fangs.

"Get back in there, nose-drip," he roared. Freddy realized that he was more scared of a real Cerberus than a mythical ghost. But only just.

He whimpered as the door slammed shut and left him in pitch-black. The man's footsteps retreated upstairs, and the upper door slammed. Freddy couldn't see a thing but shut his eyes anyway to hide from the dark. With a hammering heart, he thought of the occasions he had hidden in his tower from his furious uncle. All those times he had one friend to comfort him, one friend to talk to.

"I can be brave just like you, Dad," he whispered. "I'm not scared, I'm not scared. I'm not. I'm . . . Arrggh!"

Freddy jumped high in the air with fright as he heard the rattling of a heavy chain over the stone floor. From the dark came a terrible and ragged breath. Freddy backed away until his little backside was pushing against the wooden door. With his eyes clasped tight, he waited with trembling legs. Something, some terrible thing, was walking across the floor.

The ghost hound of Coldfax was coming for him.

A few miles away dusk fell on the woodland around Farfang Castle. A stooped and creeping figure hid among the trees. As the figure leaned forward, the fading light revealed the thick glasses and greasy hair of Dr. Foxwell Cripp. He stood licking his lips and rubbing his hands together.

"This is the place," he whispered to himself. "Who knows how many wolves are inside?" He gave a repulsive gurgle.

Just then the huge front door opened. Dr. Cripp jumped back into the shadows as Sir Hotspur strode out of the castle, his face flushed with temper. He had received a rather sharp slap on his bottom from Mrs. Mutton's wooden spoon for failing to find Freddy, and was sent yet *again* to search for him. He began to walk around the grounds pretending to look. It wasn't long before he had had enough of the charade.

"I'll keep that foolster locked up forever," he

grumbled to himself. "The Fang Council will grovel for my forgiveness. Soon I shall be hailed as the greatest of all wolves—the greatest, sir!" he roared at the night sky, and stormed inside once more.

"And I am the greatest of all men," Dr. Cripp wheezed with delight. "Tonight is the beginning. I have found them at last, and I shall not rest until Britain is free of the Fangen. Now begins the final battle against the evil werewolf pack."

He raised his silver gun dramatically to the moon and turned to face the muzzled dog tied to a tree behind him. Batty snarled defiantly as the doctor walked toward her.

Cripp gave an evil grin. "Your time will come soon enough, werewolf. You will learn to fear me."

Freddy, frozen with fear, heard the heavy breathing coming closer. Just when he felt he couldn't get any more terrified, he did. He almost barked aloud when he felt a warm breath blow over him from ghostly nostrils. The ghost hound must be only inches away. Then, at last, he could bear it no longer.

"*Yooooowwwwlllll*," Freddy howled.

He leaped high in the air as the unearthly voice of the ghost joined him.

"Yooooowwwwlllll," they howled together. Freddy turned and scratched his little toes against the heavy oak door in an effort to escape. It was useless.

"Let me out. Please let me out!" he howled in misery.

"Out. Out!" the ghost hound echoed.

A mighty paw slammed against the door just inches from him. Freddy scampered away and cringed in a corner.

After a few minutes of whimpering he noticed that everything was quiet. At last he managed to open his eyes. After several blinks the previously impenetrable darkness gradually faded into a gloomy dusk. Freddy began to hope that the ghost hound had disappeared once more. With his heart still beating rapidly, his eyes scanned the room for movement. He was confused and frightened, not only for himself, but for poor Batty too.

"I must get out of here," he yipped in frustration.

"Out. Out!" came a ghastly growl.

"Great howls!" Freddy yelped in terror once again. The ghost hound had been there all the time.

"Howls," the growl repeated.

Freddy stood looking out at the gloom, his spindly legs shivering. He could make out a dark shape lying on the floor. He made a drastic decision and summoned up every ounce of bravery he could.

"Mr. Ghost Hound?" he squeaked.

"Ghost?" came the growl again. Freddy's heart thumped, but he forced himself to continue. After all, if he had to share a dungeon with a ghost hound from hell, it would be better if they could be friends.

"Why are you here?" Freddy croaked very slowly. He wasn't too sure what to say to a phantom.

"Here . . . ?" the spirit repeated mournfully.

"What do you want?" Freddy yipped.

"Want . . . ?" the ghost echoed.

Freddy was so frustrated he forgot to be frightened.

"Stinking socks! Don't you understand anything I'm saying?" he yapped.

"I think so," came the sad reply.

"Well, I don't think you do," Freddy woofed. His courage was returning rapidly. The ghost wasn't so terrifying once you got to know him.

"How long have you been haunting here?" Freddy continued, deciding not to be frightened anymore, if that was at all possible.

"Haunting here?" the hound repeated.

"Yes. How long have you been a ghost? When were you last a living dog?" Freddy persisted, talking slowly and loudly, as one might to a deaf foreign ghost. "Why aren't you in hell?"

He jumped back in surprise when he saw the dark shape rise quickly to its feet. His terror mounted further as the hound began to walk toward him. Its chain scraped harshly against the stone floor. Freddy held his breath with fear, for now he had made a hellhound angry. Why couldn't he just keep his mouth shut? As the creature's huge head approached him, Freddy clasped his eyes tight shut again. With a terrible shiver, he felt the ghost's warm breath over him once more. After some moments of silence the creature replied quietly.

"Not a hound."

Freddy opened one eye just a little. The monster

didn't sound as if it were about to tear him limb from limb. It just sounded confused.

"I beg your pardon, sir, Mr. Ghost Hound," Freddy managed to croak politely. "I didn't mean to be rude."

"Not a hound. *Wolf*," the creature murmured, louder this time. Then he held his head high and gave a crashing roar. "I am a wolf!"

Freddy gasped with amazement and terror. He opened his eyes and saw the ghost hound clearly for the first time. He was a beautiful black wolf with brightly flashing green eyes. The great animal bounded to the oak door and pounded it with his heavy paws, and for a glorious moment the wolf's power shone through. Freddy watched with awe, but then the inner light grew faint once more and the animal slouched back onto the cold floor.

"Sorry, Mr. Ghost *Wolf* . . . I didn't realize . . . ," Freddy began.

"Why call me . . . ghost?" The wolf looked up. It began very slowly, as if trying to remember the words.

"Because I thought you were dead," Freddy said at last.

"Nearly was," the wolf murmured in agreement.

Freddy began to have a think. "So you're not dead, then?" he asked at last.

"Do I look dead?" the wolf asked reasonably.

Freddy began to feel a little foolish. "So you haven't been to hell?" he asked nervously.

"Unless this is it. Which is quite likely," the wolf said with a sorrowful laugh. His speech was becoming faster and clearer with every moment. His head and eyes were more alert too. Freddy began to feel mightily relieved and gave a silly woofy giggle.

"They told me you were dead, a *ghost hound*," he admitted.

The wolf slowly came over to look at Freddy. The poodle was still nervous but bore the inspection well, pushing his chest out proudly.

"In that case, you have been a very brave pup," the wolf replied.

Freddy felt himself grow just a little with pride. He very nearly revealed himself as a wolf too, then and there, but stopped himself just in time. He didn't want this new friend to know of his disgrace.

"What strange manner of dog are you, pup?"

the wolf wondered, peering at him through the gloom.

Freddy sighed.

"I'm a poodle," he admitted with a groan. No way did he want to reveal himself as a wolf now.

"A clever poodle," the wolf decided, and Freddy felt cheerful again already.

"Well, yes," he yipped eagerly.

"It is so long since I have met a creature who could understand Wolfen. I had almost forgotten how to speak it," the wolf replied with a nod. "I'm glad you're here."

Freddy almost burst with pride.

"But how can a *dog* speak Wolfen?" the wolf asked. "I don't understand."

"Erm? Just lucky, I suppose." Freddy didn't understand it himself; he hadn't even realized he had switched from speaking Dog to Wolfen. Language is complicated for werefolk. When in wolf form Fangen can understand a human, but in human form they can never understand a wolf. But as a dog Freddy seemed able to understand humans, dogs, and wolves. While it was extremely useful, it only served to remind him of his mixed blood, and so of his disgrace.

The wolf wasn't convinced, but Freddy didn't have time to chat.

"Well, I am glad to have met you, Mr. . . . *Wolf*, but I must try to escape now. My best friend is in terrible danger," the poodle cried.

"Escape?" The wolf laughed with a deep rumble.

"Do you think it's impossible?" Freddy asked sorrowfully.

"Nothing is easier," the wolf continued. "For you, anyway, little pup," he added sadly.

"How? If it's easy, why are you still here?" Freddy yapped in disbelief.

"I'm too large and I'm chained up. I can only go out the way I came in—through the door. And if they loosed these chains, no man or beast would stop me. I would be free and I would have my revenge!" the wolf howled, standing fierce and proud once more.

Freddy wisely stayed silent and inspected his toes. For a few moments, anyway.

"When can *I* escape, then?" he asked eventually, when it seemed the wolf had forgotten all about him. The animal was pacing strongly around the cell, now fully alert and awake.

"How about right now, little pup? Go and save yourself and your friend." He gave a smile full of sharp fangs, and his eyes glinted green. That was when Freddy saw it, hanging around the wolf's neck.

"A Moonstone!" he cried.

The wolf turned and looked at him curiously.

"It is indeed a Moonstone. How could a *poodle* know such a thing?"

The wolf leaned closer and then jolted upright. He had in turn seen the stone hanging around the little pup's neck.

"A Moonstone?" he growled. "Tell me why you wear this, pup."

As soon as Freddy had been taken from the cell, Hamish gave Bruno a secret wink. They waited until the Commander and Cerberus walked past and disappeared into the office at the far end of the long corridor. The dogs in all the cells were now very quiet, sad and fearful for the foolish pink poodle. He was only a puppy, after all. Hamish gave Bruno the nod; it was time for Bruno to unleash his secret weapon, one so dangerous that they kept it only for emergencies.

The terrier walked to the far end of the cell where he would be safe. The boxer, with a look of total innocence, moved to stand next to St. John, who was busy licking his paws. Bruno held his breath and then released the SBD. The terrible, gassy fart was indeed Silent But Deadly. St. John went green and looked close to fainting. While St. John was in this weak state and before he could cry for help, Hamish flew over and landed on his head.

"Go, quick, Bruno, find her. I can keep this fellow quiet. Phew, that's some smell you've made, lad. Well done."

Bruno smiled proudly. In an instant he had pulled up the iron grate and disappeared into the drain.

"Why do you wear the Moonstone, pup?" the huge wolf repeated softly.

"Why do you?" Freddy replied, trying to delay answering the question. The wolf sighed.

"It is a sad story of betrayal," he rasped.

"You can tell me," Freddy yapped. "I don't have to escape right now. I can wait for a few minutes, if you like."

The wolf laughed deeply. "What a funny pup you are," he answered. "Locked up with a dangerous ghost hound but happy to hang around."

"Ghost *wolf*," Freddy corrected.

The wolf lay on the stone floor and began in a soft rumble. "I am not what I seem, little poodle. Normally, I would never tell a mere dog this great secret, but I trust you not to be afraid." The wolf smiled, already fairly certain that Freddy was not "a mere dog."

Freddy preened himself happily. Of course, as soon as he saw the Moonstone, he had already guessed some of what the wolf had to tell him. But he hadn't guessed it all.

"I am no ordinary wolf, but a werewolf. Do know what that means?" The wolf paused.

"Of course I do! I'm not stupid," Freddy yipped, insulted, and the wolf laughed again.

"Of course you do," he agreed. "So normally I would be a man."

"Yes, except on the first night of the full moon," Freddy answered.

"Exactly, but when a werewolf wears a Moonstone . . ."

"You can't transform back into a man again,"

Freddy yapped furiously. "And now you have to look ridiculous forever!"

"Quite so. I must look ridiculous forever. Excellent, pup," the wolf laughed.

"Oh! I didn't mean you," Freddy said in embarrassment. "You don't look ridiculous, you look . . . fierce."

The wolf chuckled throatily once more. "Some years ago I was leading the Blood Red Hunt through the woods when my brother howled to me to come quickly to the stone circle. When I arrived, I found that Dr. Foxwell Cripp was there—the wolf hunter." The wolf hissed out the hated name. Freddy shuddered with disgust.

"It was a trap. Somehow my brother knew the hunter was there," the wolf continued.

"Your own *brother* betrayed you? What did Dr. Cripp do?" Freddy yipped.

"The pathetic wretch was trembling with fear as he held his gun. I leaped for him, but my brother knocked me from behind. Cripp never saw him in the trees. When I fell, the hunter shot me."

Freddy woofed with outrage. "With a silver bullet?" he cried. The wolf indicated yes with his ears. "How could you survive?" Freddy asked. As all werefolk know, with a silver bullet lodged in his flesh any Fangen would die quickly, for the metal is like a poison and the wound would never heal.

"The bullet passed right through my body, somehow missing all my vital organs. See the scar?"

Freddy could just make it out in the gloom, a patch of bald skin on the side of the wolf's abdomen.

"I chased Cripp down to within an inch of his terrified skin. I had lost so much blood, however, that at last I collapsed, and he escaped me. When morning arrived, I was too weak to transform back to a man. Just having the silver bullet pass through my flesh took some time to recover from. That morning, my brother, who had transformed back, found me. He put this Moonstone around my neck and brought me here. I haven't left this dungeon in six years," the wolf concluded with a sorrowful howl.

Freddy was appalled. "But why would he do that?" he cried.

"So he could be the leader of the Great Pack,"

the wolf explained. "He never forgave me for being chosen ahead of him. He is the Grand Growler now, as he informed me several years ago."

Freddy was stunned as the truth dawned on him. It was too awful, too terrible, and also too wonderful, too magnificent to be true.

"So what's your name?" Freddy bellowed.

"Flasheart, Flasheart Lupin."

Freddy couldn't speak. He couldn't dare believe it. The joy was beyond anything he had ever felt before.

"And what is your name, pup? What are you really? No mere poodle, I know that much. How do you understand Wolfen? And why do you wear a Moonstone?"

Freddy flopped onto the floor, suddenly deflated by reality. He knew that his father would be like all the other wolves and call him a disgrace. In fact, his father would be worse, for he was such a famously brave wolf, so proud of the memory of Sir Rathbone. He would be ashamed to have a son like him. There was no escaping it. Freddy gave a huge sigh and began.

"I'm supposed to be a werewolf like you," he

said sadly, waiting for his father to laugh out loud or roar with disgust. When he didn't, Freddy carried on.

"I don't know why I'm not. I never wanted to be a poodle, but when I transformed, I looked like this. Only not pink, and with no silly bald patches. My cousins did that, and I'm still going to get them for it. Anyway . . . the Fang Council was furious with me and expelled me from the Great Pack."

The wolf was silent for some moments. "So they sent you here to Coldfax?" he growled. "That's no way to treat a pup."

"Nobody sent me; I was caught. But the worst thing is that Cripp is here. I've seen him, and I must escape and warn the Great Pack. And he took my friend, even though I tried to save her. And when I bit him, and stole his Moonstone, they threw me down here so that you could eat me . . . and . . . and . . ." Freddy paused for breath as it all tumbled out. "And I tried to warn my uncle, but he says I must stay here forever. He hates me because I've brought shame upon my pack and disgrace to the memory of . . . of . . ." Freddy paused and closed his eyes in shame; the moment he had been trying to avoid had arrived. ". . . Sir Rathbone de Lupinne," he croaked.

More silence followed, and then at last the wolf crept closer. He sniffed the little poodle, whose eyes were now hidden under his paws. Then came a deep growl.

"Freddy?" the wolf asked. Freddy didn't want to look up and see the disappointment in his father's green eyes. He said yes with his tail.

"I am the father of the bravest pup in the world." The wolf's voice was deep.

Freddy looked up in astonishment. "You're not ashamed of me, then?" he cried.

"I have never been prouder or happier in my life," his father replied huskily.

"Oh, Dad, I've missed you so much," Freddy yipped.

Within a second, Freddy was being crushed between the great paws of the mighty wolf as father and son were reunited. Because Freddy is very sensitive about being considered a sissy, we will leave them alone to their tears and hugs for a short while.

CHAPTER SEVENTEEN

THE PLAN MASTER

"Good shot," Flasheart roared with delight.

"I told Mrs. Mutton you'd say that," his son laughed.

"Lady Whitehorn was always too snooty anyway," Flasheart laughed. He had, of course, just heard about the infamous "Hotspur in the pond" incident.

A magnificent change had come over the wolf since discovering Freddy's identity. His air of melancholy had dropped away, and the sorrows of the past six years seemed to weigh lightly upon his heart. Freddy had quickly related to his father all of his adventures since his Transwolfation.

Flasheart had not been able to shed much light on Freddy's poodle status. He did know, however, that the aunt's poodle, Dripsy-Wimpsy, had bitten Freddy's mother when she was pregnant. That much was certain.

"Somehow you must have canine as well as Fangen blood," his father said. "But I can't imagine one bite was enough to challenge the bloodline of Sir Rathbone himself. No, there is a deeper mystery here, pup, but one for another time. For now we have more urgent business."

"Why did it have to happen to me?" Freddy whined.

"Don't be too upset about it," Flasheart decided. "We wouldn't have found each other again otherwise."

"Yeah," Freddy yapped, "but I'd still rather have been a fierce wolf when I found you."

"Being fierce is not the same thing as being brave," his father advised, and gave him a friendly nudge on the ears. Freddy was knocked right over by the force.

"If you were a wolf, you'd be too big to escape." Flasheart stood up. "Freddy, we have two ruthless enemies: Cripp and Hotspur. But you must go—for me, for Batty, but most of all for the werefolk of Britain. If Cripp finds the Wolfen

Names, we are all lost. You are the only one who can save the werefolk."

"Okay . . . I'll do my best." Freddy gulped.

"Now, time to escape," Flasheart roared. He dragged his chain over the floor toward the farthest and darkest corner of the dungeon. There he pointed at a square hole in the stone floor. It was like the one in Freddy's old cell, only this one was half the size and didn't have a grate over it. It was just big enough for a small poodle to slither down.

Looking down into the small black hole, Freddy felt terrible about leaving his father. He remembered his own earlier escape plan, and an exciting idea started to form in his poodle-y head.

"Dad," he said quickly, "would you be able to break my chain? So I can transform back?"

Flasheart gave a chuckle. "Of course I can, Freddy. I am a great and powerful beast, remember," the wolf replied. You can begin to see from whom Freddy had inherited his vanity. "But if you transform into a boy, you will be trapped too. You won't be able to fit down the drain, and the door is bolted on the outside."

"But I won't transform, not straightaway,"

Freddy woofed excitedly. "I have Cripp's Moonstone ring inside me. It's brilliant." He told the wolf his plan.

"There is too much danger. What if you run into Cerberus?" Flasheart said doubtfully.

"I am *not* leaving you here," Freddy yapped crossly. "I can let you out and still save Batty. I know I can."

The wolf smiled slowly. "Then we have to act quickly." He rose and padded softly over to the poodle. He carefully placed his great fangs around the Moonstone chain.

"It will work, won't it, Dad?" Freddy said softly. "The ring in my stomach will stop me from transforming?"

"I hope so; otherwise, we are all lost," the wolf replied, his green eyes glinting.

"Tails crossed, then," Freddy said. The wolf bit down on the chain. For a second it tightened horribly around Freddy's neck, and then it shattered. The chain and its Moonstone clattered to the floor. Freddy felt a great surge of relief.

"Ha-ha-hardy-ha," he yapped triumphantly. "Oh wait, oh no! Oh no!" he cried in a panic.

"What, Freddy? Are you transforming? Quickly,

pick up the Moonstone again." The wolf looked urgently on the floor for the chain as Freddy rolled around. Then with a cheeky yip the poodle jumped up again.

"Only joking," Freddy laughed.

"Not funny, young pup," the wolf growled angrily.

"Sorry." Freddy tried his best to look genuinely sorry. The wolf was not convinced but was still in a good enough humor not to mind much.

"Well now," Flasheart said, "time to go."

Freddy took a large gulp for courage and put his nose down the drain. Ignoring the nervous feeling in his stomach, he slid down into the dark.

The narrow tunnels were pitch-black and there was revolting slime all over the floor. The ceiling dripped oily black water and several of the tunnels were alive with rats. They scurried and leaped over one another to escape the approaching dog.

Freddy couldn't find the smells he was searching for. He did, however, find the exit, where the drain ran out of a large hole in the fort's high wall. It was about ten feet above the ground outside and would have been easy enough to jump from, except that it was sealed with a heavy iron grille. Not even Bruno would be able to break a hole in it. The only way out of Coldfax was through the front door. Freddy smelled the cold night air and could see the moon high in the sky. It made his Fangen blood tingle; how he wanted to run across the night under those warm moonbeams!

Ahead of him in the tunnel a dark shape was panting in the shadows.

"Arrgggh!"

Freddy nearly jumped out of his skin as the dark shadow screamed in terror. "Bruno?" he yipped into the gloom.

"Stinky?" a gruff voice replied with relief. "I thought you was the ghost hound."

"I thought you were Cerberus," Freddy laughed. For once the two dogs were pleased to see each other.

"I'm off to save Batty," the boxer barked. "We thought you was a goner."

"Change of plan. We can't get out that way," Freddy replied. "Come on, we have to run."

Hamish nearly dropped St. John's ear when he saw Bruno's head emerge from the open drain.

He was lying across the spaniel's head and held the poor dog's ear ransom in his mouth.

"Look who I found," Bruno gruffed. "Stinky."

Hamish jumped up in astonishment when the poodle's curly pink head emerged next. "Freddy! How? What? When? Where?" he woofed.

St. John instantly jumped up in outrage and opened his muzzle wide to woof. It was immediately clamped shut again by Bruno's heavy paw.

"One woof, Champion, and not even Cerberus will be able to save you," the boxer hissed menacingly. The spaniel glared with hatred but sank down again silently.

"I came out through the drain," Freddy yipped excitedly.

"What about the ghost hound? Did you see him?" Hamish asked eagerly.

"He's not a hound, he's a wolf," Freddy yipped.

"A wolf?" the dogs howled in dismay.

Freddy had no time to waste.

"I've something important to tell you. I know you won't believe a word of it, but just listen anyway. Then when it happens, you'll know what to do. Agreed?" He looked at the two dogs. They nodded their ears.

"Now, I've told you before that I'm a wolf."

Hamish and Bruno immediately raised their hairy eyebrows at each other. Freddy was right, they weren't going to believe a single word, but he took a deep breath and began.

"Well, I'm a wolf who is really a human boy. . . ."

Hamish snorted and Bruno laughed out loud. Freddy ignored them and plowed on right to the end of his plan.

"Now, here are the things you have to remember. When I am a boy, I won't understand you and you won't understand me. The wolf will understand me but not you. I won't understand him and neither will you. Do you understand?"

"No, lad," Hamish replied.

"Not a woof," Bruno sniggered.

St. John looked up from under Bruno's paw and rolled his eyes at their stupidity.

"Oh, never mind. Look, when I'm a boy, just follow me. It will work, I promise! Hamish, can you run on your sore paw?" Freddy looked with concern at the injury that Cerberus had given the terrier.

"No chance, lad. You'd best leave me behind and just think of finding that brave lass in time."

"No, we're not leaving any dog behind in this terrible place." Freddy shook his head. "When I give you this signal"—he balanced on his hind legs, held up his front paws, and winked—"organize the dogs into two groups. Bruno, you lead the fast ones and we'll go and find Batty. Hamish, you bring the others to meet us near the House of Howls, in the woods of the Red Wolf. Do you know it?"

The other two dogs looked at him in dismay.

"Aye, but Freddy, that's an unnatural place. . . ."

"Yeah, it's my home," the pup interrupted. "It's where Cripp will have taken her. Whatever happens, don't let anyone escape from the castle, no matter who they are. We have to go *now*, so are you ready?"

"Are we ever!" Bruno cried.

Freddy walked toward the drain in the center of the floor. He looked back at the cell door. There was the twelve-inch gap at the top. He was going to escape from Coldfax, and what was more, he was going help his father escape too.

"Now, I'm just going back down in the hole for *you know what*. Don't worry, I can fit through this drain again as a boy; it's bigger than the one in the wolf's cell. Okay?"

Hamish and Bruno looked at each other and shrugged. In a second the crazed poodle had jumped down the drain once more. He had a big job to see to. Hamish and Bruno politely turned their backs to the hole, and the terrier began to murmur softly.

"Just tell me if I have this right, lad. . . . Freddy will have a poo, and so will *remove* the ring of moon from his bowels."

"That's right, he's going to poo the ring out." Bruno nodded.

"Then he will magically transform into a human boy and release us all from Coldfax?" Hamish looked at his cellmate.

"Here we go," Freddy's voice called up.

The two dogs couldn't help themselves. They looked at each other and collapsed with helpless tears of howling laughter. The poor pup was totally and utterly unhinged.

"False alarm—just a fart," laughed Freddy.

Hamish thought of Batty and shook his head sorrowfully.

"Ha!"

They turned toward the open grate to see the head and shoulders of Freddy Lupin, human boy, emerge with a smile of triumph. He punched the air.

"The Plan Master!" he whispered in delight.

All three dogs yelped and jumped in the air with fright.

"My hairy ears!" Hamish croaked.

Bruno threw back his head and howled in confusion.

"Shush, shush, you'll fetch Cerberus," Freddy whispered urgently.

His hair, no longer curly, stood on end as ridiculously as it ever had. It wasn't black, however, but a most putrid shade of pink. His happy green eyes sparkled as he grinned.

He climbed out of the drain. The dogs backed away suspiciously.

"Come on, boys, it's me." He held out his hands for the dogs to smell.

Hamish and Bruno inched forward nervously, sniffed, looked at each other, and sniffed again. Freddy laughed. He saw their tails wagging madly and understood; they were laughing too.

Now—escape.

Freddy stuck first his nose, then his ear through the iron bars of the cell door. As far as he could tell, Cerberus wasn't around, but he needed to act quickly. He caught a glimpse of St. John sneaking to the back of the cell. He was not to be trusted. In a second Freddy had dropped the outraged spaniel into the drain and replaced the iron grate. They heard the Supreme Champion fall with a gentle splash into the slime below. He howled in fury. The other two dogs wagged their tails merrily.

"Here I go," Freddy whispered.

He placed a foot on the lock and heaved himself up the iron bars. His head and shoulders touched the ceiling. Freddy's whole plan hinged on his being able to squeeze through the gap. It was tight and awkward, but his head and shoulders went through, then his arms and chest.

"Farts!" Freddy grunted. He was balanced in a most precarious position. He was nearly upside down, with his chest and head dangling outside the bars. His bottom and legs were wedged against the ceiling.

If he was lucky, he could just about nudge his way out. . . .

"Oh no, oh no . . ."

He crashed onto the corridor floor with a heavy

thud but managed not to groan. He turned and saw Hamish's and Bruno's beaming smiles and wagging tails. He was out!

"So far, so brilliant," he whispered. He gave them a grin and began creeping down the corridor. Despite the noise, the dogs in the other cells seemed to be fast asleep. Freddy held his breath as he tiptoed along the walkway to the Commander's office. To his left was the main iron door, through which he and Batty had entered on their first day. In it was a smaller wooden door with a flap.

Ho ho, Cerberus! Freddy thought. This was obviously how the guard dog came and went. There was a bolt on the flap, which Freddy quickly locked.

He felt less nervous now that Cerberus had been dealt with so easily. Slowly he opened the office door and peeped inside. The room was dark and silent, but from beyond another door came the sound of a television. With his heart beating fast, Freddy reached for the light switch and turned it on.

"So far, not so hard." He laughed to himself with relief. "Now, the keys! Where are the keys?"

Freddy opened and closed drawers and cupboards, but he couldn't find any keys. He turned to face a painting on the wall, a cutesy picture of fluffy puppies flopped onto flowers.

"Why would a mean old lady who hates dogs have that on her wall? Unless . . ."

Freddy reached up and pulled aside the painting. Behind it was a hidden cupboard.

"Unless it's a decoy." He smiled as he saw a large collection of keys. Each one had a piece of tape with a cell number written on it. There was also a larger, older, heavier key with no label, and with it a much smaller one.

From outside came a heavy thump followed by an almighty roar of anger.

"Great howls," Freddy breathed. "Cerberus."

The wolfhound had not been pleased to discover his door was locked by running headlong into it. Freddy heard a door click behind him and felt a rush of panic. He turned to see the Commander point at him and scream. Freddy ran and fell over a small table with a crash.

"A burglar. A naked burglar," she gasped.

"Naked?" Freddy cried, looking down in horror. He quickly snatched up a cushion and covered

himself. He had spent so long as a dog he had completely forgotten about his clothes.

"Please, don't panic! I'm not a burglar, I'm a poodle," he protested, trying to calm the frantic woman.

"I'm calling the police," the Commander cried before racing back into the other room and slamming the door closed. Freddy jumped into action and wedged a wooden chair tightly under the door handle.

"That should keep her in. Now I'm going to end up in human jail!" he muttered to himself.

Freddy had to act quickly if he meant to release his father and still get to Farfang Castle in time to stop Cripp. He looked down the long corridor. The coast was clear. He could see all the dog's muzzles poking through the bars on either side. He began to run down to the dungeon door at the far end. By now all the dogs were awake and alert, and volleys of barks followed as he passed. Unknown to him, the word was spreading. Hamish and Bruno barked to their neighbors and they to theirs.

"He's the poodle."

"The pink one?"

"A boy?"

"And a wolf."

"How?"

"No one knows."

Freddy reached the door that led down to the dungeon. As he did, he heard a mighty crash behind him and turned in terror to see Cerberus at the far end of the corridor, the door flap smashed open. The wolfhound saw the boy with the pink hair, smelled the air, and understood. St. John had been right. He gave a savage grin.

"Great howls!" Freddy gasped. He turned to try the large old key in the lock, but in his panic dropped it. The dogs began to bark in warning as Cerberus ran past them toward Freddy. The cries were almost deafening, but above them all Freddy could hear the hideous scrape of claws on stone behind him.

Freddy reached for the key.

With a roar of hatred Cerberus leaped into the air.

Freddy turned the lock and slipped through the door just before the wolfhound slammed into it. The force of the dog's body banged the door closed and threw the boy down the slippery, cold stairs. He landed with a groan at the bottom, the keys still clutched tightly in his trembling hand.

"So far, so terrifying," he squeaked in relief, and dragged himself shakily to his feet.

Freddy found a light switch in the dark stairwell. A weak yellow glow illuminated the solid door that led to the dungeon below. Freddy tugged at the bolt with all his might.

The wolf beyond gave a low growl.

"Don't worry, Dad, it's me!" Freddy cried in triumph as the bolt shot back and he pushed open the dungeon door.

There, blinking in the light, stood his father, his tail wagging proudly. Now Freddy could see how badly the wolf had suffered. He was still huge, but thinner than he should have been. Strong streaks of gray lay in his otherwise jet-black coat.

"So far, so great." Freddy walked forward nervously. The wolf lunged at him, and Freddy gave a cry as he was pushed to the ground. The wolf's fangs reached for him. . . . Flasheart licked his forehead and with a heavy paw ruffled his hair. The wolf gave a deep, rasping laugh.

"Very funny!" Freddy said grumpily, but then laughed too.

They were interrupted by the sound of distant sirens.

"The police!" Freddy cried. "We have to go, Dad."

He walked to the wall where the wolf's heavy chain was padlocked to a metal ring. With a silent prayer Freddy tried the smaller key. It fit perfectly! He laughed with relief, and the wolf howled loudly as the huge padlock fell easily to the floor. With some difficulty Freddy pulled the chain out of the hoop on the wolf's collar, and at last Flasheart was free. He paced around the small room, flexing his stiff muscles.

"Dad, Cerberus is outside waiting for us," Freddy whispered nervously. "Do you understand?"

The wolf flicked his ears. *Yes*.

Freddy looked at his father with concern. He was bigger than Cerberus, but thin, and who knew how much weakened by his years in the dungeon.

The wolf pushed Freddy aside with his muzzle and nodded urgently at the door. Freddy reached forward and opened it quickly.

* * *

Hamish and Bruno and all the other dogs were straining their muzzles through the bars of their cells to see.

Cerberus was standing and glaring at the door—waiting, just waiting. He knew there was no other way out for the poodle-boy, and he was going to tear him limb from limb. An extra worry heightened the tension among the other dogs. They all believed that beyond the door the ghost hound stalked. The poodle-boy had to emerge soon, and then what would happen?

Without warning the door flew open. The dogs barked and Cerberus growled. They all expected to see a frightened human pup.

Instead, Flasheart Lupin, the great black wolf, leaped out with a terrifying snarl. Cerberus jumped back in shock. The dogs yapped and howled in fright and confusion. Even Hamish and Bruno, who had been told what to expect, could hardly believe it.

"The ghost hound! The ghost hound!" howled the other crazed dogs.

Cerberus knew better than that, of course—he knew about the wolf below. He soon recovered, and the two huge beasts snarled at each other. Flasheart was the larger animal, but Cerberus was heavy, well fed, mean, and strong. Freddy watched with a pounding heart from behind the half-closed door.

"Be careful, Dad," he whispered to himself.

Cerberus flung himself at the wolf, and the two animals rolled over in a dangerous and savage embrace. Freddy heard the police siren again, nearer this time. With no time to waste, he carefully inched past the fighting beasts and ran toward his old cell. He opened the door, and Hamish and Bruno ran out.

Freddy turned back to see his father limping, blood running from a deep wound in one of his rear legs. Cerberus was tensed, ready for another attack.

"Dad, lead him here," he called. Flasheart turned around so that he was nearer to the cell. He began to walk backward toward Freddy. Seeing his prey retreating, Cerberus flung himself at the wolf once again, and the pair rolled over. Inch by inch Flasheart pushed the wolfhound toward the open cell door.

When they were close enough, Freddy cried

out, "Hey, Cerberus, bite this!" He waggled his bare backside at his enemy.

Cerberus turned toward the boy in outrage, and as he did, the wolf lunged and knocked the guard dog into the cell. Freddy slammed the door. In a fury Cerberus threw himself against the bars, and Flasheart pushed back. Cerberus howled in outrage. Freddy struggled with the lock, but the door wouldn't close. Bruno and Hamish flung themselves against the bars, and finally the door snapped shut.

"We've done it!" Freddy cried in triumph.

Cerberus snarled and spat from behind the bars as Freddy flung his arms around the wounded wolf's neck. All the dogs erupted into barks and howls. Freddy didn't need to understand the woofs to know they were cheering. Cerberus was where he belonged at last.

At that moment Dr. Cripp was crossing the bridge that led across the moat of Farfang Castle. He crept over, his heart beating fast with anticipation. Quickly he scurried into the shadows of the high walls. Cripp jumped back in fright as the heavy oak door creaked open.

"Go on, then, do it. You daren't!" a young boy's voice whispered.

"Of course I dare, dunderbrain!" answered a girl.

The next moment a plump, pink, redheaded girl ran out of the castle and onto the bridge. She had a bundle of clean laundry in her arms, and she threw it into the water of the moat below. The boy peeked his head out from the door and shrieked with delight as he saw several pairs of Mrs. Mutton's enormous great knickers floating away. They had just made a raid on the house-keeper's ironing pile. The twins roared with laughter at their prank and then disappeared inside. The door, however, did not quite close behind them, and after a furtive glance Dr. Cripp opened it and stepped inside the castle. He took a coil of wire from his pocket and set about lay-ing his snares. Tonight he would begin the final destruction of the Fangen. A slow smile slid across his sweating face.

CHAPTER EIGHTEEN: BREAKOUT

While Cerberus snarled venomously from his cell, Freddy released all the other dogs. He then held up his two thumbs to Hamish and Bruno and winked, just as he'd promised. The terrier barked out instructions to the dogs around him. Quickly the noisy rabble organized into two columns. The oldest, smallest, and slowest dogs stood behind Hamish. Bruno, looking proud and eager, marshaled the fastest, fittest animals. As they passed him, Cerberus flung himself against the bars, looking hungry for vengeance on Freddy. The boy just laughed at him and once again waggled his bare backside. Cerberus's reign was over at last.

"Okay, Dad?" Freddy called.

Flasheart walked slowly up the corridor, and the dogs parted around him in awe. Hamish had explained by now that he wasn't a ghost hound but a wolf. Not just a wolf, but one twice the size of any normal wolf. Usually he would be an animal to be feared and hated, but he had overcome the dreaded Cerberus and helped them to escape. The dogs were nervous but respectful of him.

Freddy unbolted the outside door, and as he did he saw the Commander's raincoat hanging nearby. It was, of course, pink.

"Well, it is my color," he laughed as he slipped it on. It wouldn't do to be seen naked in Milford.

"Okay, here we go," he called nervously, and flung open the door. The police were waiting. Their flashlights flooded the courtyard with light.

The portcullis that guarded the entrance to Coldfax Fort was firmly shut.

"Wait here, Dad, while I see how to open it. When I give the signal, charge as fast as you can."

Flasheart flapped his ears in reply. Bruno and Hamish kept their columns behind the wolf. Freddy ran toward a small door next to the portcullis.

A policeman spotted him immediately. "Hey, you there!"

"Sorry, can't stop," Freddy called.

"Sergeant Green here. Open this door. Immediately," the policeman called.

Ignoring him, Freddy ducked inside. It wasn't hard to see how to open the gate. A heavy chain was wrapped around a wheel and then disappeared up into the ceiling. It was connected to a motor with a red button and a green button.

"So far, so easy-peasy," he laughed.

Freddy pushed the green button. The engine started to hum as it rattled to life, and the chain went tight around the wheel. Freddy ran back outside to see if anything had happened.

"Open this gate this instant!" the policeman was now roaring.

"I'm trying to," Freddy said. He stood in the center of the courtyard with the lights trained upon him and watched the portcullis anxiously. If it didn't open, they would never get away. With a huge creaking groan the chain began to winch the heavy iron grille up. Once under way, it began to rise rapidly.

"Now, sonny. What are you doing in there?"

the policeman asked as he waited for the gate to rise.

"Breaking out." Freddy smiled, his pink hair blowing in the wind.

The policeman laughed. "I'm afraid I can't give you permission to do that, son."

"That's okay. I'm not asking for it," Freddy replied. He was an outlaw to make Batty proud.

"Now, Dad. Go! Go!" he called at the top of his voice.

"Not one dog is leaving these premises . . . ," the sergeant said sternly. Then his face dropped in horrible surprise.

Flying toward him across the courtyard was a huge and savage black wolf followed by an army of dogs, all barking and snarling like wild beasts.

"Charge!" Freddy cried, running toward the opening gate.

"Close the gate! Close the gate!" the other police officers called in panic.

"Too late! Run away, run away!"

The terrified officers ran around trying to escape. Two tried to climb into the same car door but only succeeded in colliding with each other and falling back onto the ground. Another two took off into the woods. Sergeant Green stood frozen with terror as the enormous wolf approached him. He gave a rising cry as the animal halted at his feet. The wolf gave a fiendish grin, its green eyes glinting, as Freddy jumped onto its back.

"Not *one* dog is leaving, but a *hundred* are," Freddy laughed.

The huge wolf howled at the moon. The poor sergeant had had enough; he turned tail and took off at full speed into the woods.

"We did it! We did it!" Freddy roared in triumph. "I *am* the Plan Master!"

Some time later the light of the moon shone down upon a pack of dogs streaming over fields and through woods. Freddy sat astride Flasheart, holding on for all he was worth as the huge animal leaped over ditches and dikes, hardly slowed by his injury. The heat from the moonbeams was already healing the wound on the great wolf's leg, and his old strength was returning. The gray streaks in his fur were fading as his Fangen blood pulsed. Behind them Bruno led his column of fighting-fit dogs through the night. They hurtled toward Farfang Castle, Sir Hotspur, and Dr. Cripp, toward danger and a friend in need.

"We're coming, Batty," Freddy called. "We're coming at last!"

The charge halted a few yards short of the stone wall around Farfang Castle. Freddy's tower was silhouetted against the moonlit sky. The dogs collapsed on the ground for a moment to recover their breath. Freddy jumped off his father's back and felt a rush of relief to be home again. The grounds of Farfang were well secured to keep out nosy neighbors. This gate could be opened from the outside only by typing a code into the electronic keypad. However, a strange-looking device with flashing neon signals had been attached to the controls, and the gate was open slightly. Someone had broken in. *Cripp!* Urgently Freddy pushed the gate wide, and the dogs filed through.

Flasheart raised his nose and sniffed the night air, smelling his home for the first time in six years. He put back his ears and howled. Dark clouds were dragging across the moon. The air was colder and the wind was rising. The wolf's howls echoed eerily through the air. Bruno and the other dogs paused and looked at one another, then raced forward and into the grounds of the House of Howls.

In his study Sir Hotspur awoke with a start. His newspaper had fallen over his head.

"Flasheart?" he croaked.

There was no mistaking that howl. He jumped up quickly and glared out the window.

"I warned you *never* to return to Farfang!"

He reached inside a desk drawer and took out a tiny gun.

"Cripp isn't the only one with silver bullets."

"Bruno, here boy," Freddy called.

The boxer approached suspiciously. All the dogs were extremely nervous being there, on the grounds of the Red Wolf. Batty was right; they all knew and feared this place.

"Find Batty," Freddy hissed urgently, pointing his finger toward the woods. Bruno only looked at him in confusion. Freddy groaned and for once wished he was a dog again.

"Batty! Batty! Find!" he repeated loudly.

Just when there seemed no chance of getting through to the dim hound, the boxer's ears pinged high. In a second he had barked out instructions to his companions. The dogs immediately ran in all directions. Freddy breathed in relief that Bruno had understood. With his nose on the ground, the boxer began to move slowly toward the castle. On the lawn he picked up a trail and barked excitedly. Flasheart and Freddy followed him as he took off at top speed into the woods. They ran into a clearing behind the castle, and Flasheart growled in fury.

"Is she here, Dad?" Freddy whispered, his stomach aching with nerves. It was now hours since Cripp had taken Batty. Who knew what the evil hunter might have done to her?

Drops of heavy rain began to fall. Just then Bruno appeared on the edge of the clearing and gave an urgent gruff. Freddy and his father followed as he jumped back into a dark thicket. There in the gloom, Freddy could make out a small furry body lying motionless on the ground. He crept forward, dreading what it might be. Bruno was whimpering pathetically and pushing his nose against it.

"Batty?" Freddy called gently, but there was no response.

As he drew nearer, he was overpowered by the most repulsive stench. Flasheart stopped immediately and howled in pain. Several bundles of a green herb with dull yellow flowers were strewn around the still animal.

"*Wolfsbane!*" Freddy cried. The stench was worse than a thousand rotten egg farts. The wolf wouldn't move a step nearer, for to his sensitive nose it was practically poisonous. Freddy held his breath and kicked the bundles as far away as he could.

He then crept forward and knelt down next to Batty. The muzzle was still over her mouth, and her lead was tied to a tree. She didn't seem to be breathing.

"Oh, Batty!" Freddy cried, tears pooling in his eyes. "I'm too late. I'm so sorry."

How could that hateful man have killed such a beautiful dog? Batty's long black-and-white hair had fallen over her eyes. Freddy pushed it away and hugged his best friend.

A wet tongue reached out from the muzzle and licked Freddy's cheek.

"Batty?" he cried in wonderment.

The mongrel's pretty eyes opened briefly and then closed again, and she began to snore contentedly.

Freddy hooted with relief. He spotted a tissue on the ground nearby and picked it up. There was some sort of chemical on it.

"She's been *drugged*," he cried in delight. "She's only asleep, Dad. She's okay." He hugged the dozing mongrel tightly once again.

With a sudden growl, Flasheart turned around and stared intently into the gloom. Someone or something was coming. Bruno gave a bark and bravely jumped forward to investigate. He heard a sound and raced off into the woods in pursuit. Flasheart nudged his son in warning, and Freddy shook Batty urgently. The tired mongrel woke up reluctantly and tried to bare her teeth, but the muzzle prevented it. She sniffed Freddy and looked at his pink hair, and her eyes suddenly flashed to life. She jumped up in delight and wagged her tail madly.

"Yes, it's me!" Freddy laughed quickly. "But shush, girl, someone's coming. Dad, is it Cripp?"

Freddy untied Batty's muzzle and released her. The huge wolf turned to face Batty, who flinched in terror. Flasheart gently licked her forehead, while Batty stared in amazement. She looked at Freddy and realized that whoever the wolf was, he must be a friend. Nervously, she held out her paw as Freddy had taught her. Flasheart took it in his and the two wagged their tails happily. She really was the bravest mongrel Freddy had ever seen.

The three companions ran quickly toward Farfang Castle. Flasheart kept looking behind him in concern, but they reached the door in safety. The rain was now falling heavily. The door was slightly open, as Dr. Cripp had left it.

"Let's get inside," Freddy whispered. "We can find something to get your chain off with."

The wolf and mongrel nipped inside. Freddy entered last and pushed the door closed with all his strength. It slammed behind him with a horrible bang that echoed throughout Farfang Castle. Their arrival had been announced.

Bruno's chase had led to nothing. He returned to the lawn in time to see Batty run inside and flopped onto the grass in relief. He barked out the news to the other dogs, and they soon joined him. They would wait there in case Freddy needed them.

Freddy led his father and friend up to the tower room and then sneaked downstairs. He hunted about in the workroom near the kitchen and then sprinted back up the spiral staircase.

Ten minutes later the wolf inspected his chain collar in the mirror. The Moonstone shone back at him mockingly. Freddy had tried bashing it with a hammer, picking it out with a nail file, and sawing through the chain, all to no avail.

"The key must be in Uncle Hotspur's study. He

put the padlock on you, so he must have the key. I'm going to look for it."

The wolf flicked his ears doubtfully. He knew it would be dangerous.

"Well, it's worth a try." Freddy jumped up.

The wolf rose to come too.

"No, Dad. You have to stay here. I'll be okay. Even if he heard the door slam shut, Uncle Hotspur wouldn't know it's us in the castle. If he catches me, you'll still be safe; he thinks you're in Coldfax. Promise to stay hidden."

The wolf reluctantly flicked his tail in agreement.

Freddy scooted down the spiral stairs and paused at the bottom to listen carefully. The old stone passage leading to the main part of the castle was silent. With a racing heart, he ran for it. He passed the kitchen and there, straight ahead of him, was the door that led to the famous pond. Freddy opened it and peeped out. The square courtyard was empty. Rain was falling from the dark clouds above. It splashed into the ornamental pond. Above him a thunderclap boomed. Freddy sprinted out. By cutting across the courtyard to the far side of the castle, he could avoid walking past the Red Stairs. He was drenched when he reached the opposite door, which squeaked horribly when Freddy opened it.

"Great howls," he muttered. "Why does every door squeak when I need it to be quiet?"

He was right outside the door to Uncle Hotspur's study. Freddy looked up and down the dark corridor. Everything was quiet.

"Okay! Here we go. . . ."

Freddy ran toward the study door but immediately tripped. He flew through the air and torpedoed headfirst through the door.

"Ow!" he yelped.

Freddy rolled into a small table. He knocked off a delicate vase, which smashed nicely onto his head.

"*Ow!*" he yelped again. If he had used a megaphone to announce his arrival back in the castle, it would have made less noise. He turned to see what had tripped him. A tight string was stretched across the doorway.

"A booby trap!" he whispered. But who had laid it? Dr. Cripp? Uncle Hotspur? With a horrid, creepy feeling that someone was watching him,

Freddy jumped up and began to search through Uncle Hotspur's drawers. He wanted to find that key as quickly as possible and get away from whoever had set the trap.

"Where is it?" he groaned in frustration.

"Looking for this, sir?"

Freddy yelped as his uncle's dreaded voice boomed out from the doorway behind him. He swung around to see Sir Hotspur holding up a small steel key, his eyes glinting furiously. He held the silver gun in his other hand. Freddy's face fell at the sight of it.

"It wasn't me!" he croaked uselessly.

"But it was you, sir. And this *key* stays with me. Flasheart will never be a man again. Not ever!"

"Traitor! You've broken the Pact of the Fangen," Freddy cried. "All werefolk are supposed to protect their pack—not . . . lock them up, not *shoot* them!"

"You dare call me traitor? A poodle that has polluted the blood of Sir Rathbone? I'll teach you, sir."

Sir Hotspur raised his gun and took aim. Freddy picked up a cushion and threw it at his uncle, but Sir Hotspur flung it away with a snarl and stepped forward. With a roar of surprise he tripped over into the room.

"What in the name of All Howls?" Sir Hotspur cried as he crashed to the floor. The booby trap had struck again. Freddy jumped high with fright as his uncle rolled toward him. The small key flew from his grasp, and with a cry of delight Freddy jumped for it.

"No, sir!" Hotspur roared, grabbing the boy's ankle. The key lay just beyond Freddy's reach. As he kicked and strained for it, Sir Hotspur began pulling him back slowly. Just then he gave a bellow of pain and anger and released Freddy, who jumped up, the key grasped safely in his hand.

He turned in triumph to see Batty's teeth firmly embedded in Uncle Hotspur's large backside. The outraged man roared in fury but couldn't remove her.

"Nobody messes with *this* wolf and his friends!" Freddy yelled.

He jumped over his uncle and ran to the door.

"Okay, Batty, release that fat bum," he called back. The mongrel did, with a growl of distaste.

The two friends didn't wait to see the furious

man rise but sped back across the rainy courtyard. Behind them they heard the mighty roar of
Sir Hotspur Lupin in pursuit.

He was an extremely angry werewolf, and he
still held the silver gun in his hand.

Freddy and Batty charged up the spiral stairs to the tower. Freddy rushed in, but Batty, concerned about Sir Hotspur's pursuit, stayed outside to guard.

"Dad, I've got it!" Freddy shouted as he crashed into his room. His father wasn't there.

Instead, he was greeted by the pink piggy smiles of Harriet and Chariot.

"What are *you* doing here? Where's the wolf?" he cried.

"*Wolf?*" Harriet snorted. "No wolf in England would be seen with you, Dripsy-Wimpsy."

"Hey, Barbie boy, nice hair," Chariot giggled like a pig.

Freddy was not the boy, or poodle, he had been the last time he saw the Putrid Pair. He had much bigger problems to worry about than their teasing . . . saving the whole of Wolfenkind being just one of them.

"Clear off," he ordered. "Dad, come out quick! They're just Weren, just babies," he called, hoping his father was near.

The terrible twins didn't approve of this at all. It was so unlike Freddy to be calm under fire. From below came Sir Hotspur's shouts.

"I'm coming, sir. I'm coming," he bellowed.

"Oh, vomitous puke," Freddy groaned. He heard his uncle's heavy feet slamming upon the stone steps.

"He's up here, Dad. Don't worry, we've got him!" Harriet called down.

"Keep quiet, butt-brain, he's gone mad!" Freddy told her. "He's broken the Pact of the Fangen. He's a danger to all werefolk."

"What's the matter, Wimpsy? Scared of my da . . . ?" Her voice trailed away. She pointed in terror at the huge black wolf that had emerged from under the bed. Flasheart had hidden so as not to frighten the children.

"Who's that?" Chariot trembled and took a step backward.

"*My* dad!" Freddy cried in triumph. "Why, are you scared of *him*?" he laughed. "Now clear off, *puppies*, this is wolves' work."

Freddy had the key in his hand but could hear Uncle Hotspur approaching rapidly. There wasn't enough time to unlock his father's chain. He had a spark of inspiration.

"The Slide of Doom!" he cried.

In an instant he had pulled out the large metal tray. The wolf leaped onto it with a twinkle in his eye; he had always loved this ride. Freddy began to push it toward the steps with some difficulty.

"No way, Dripsy-Wimpsy," Harriet cried. She started pulling at Freddy's pink raincoat.

"*Ger-off-me*, can't you see I'm busy?" he complained, trying to shake her off.

Once again he was saved by Batty. She charged into the room from the top of the stairs, barking ferociously, and backed Harriet and Chariot into the corner as if they were a couple of timid, porky pink sheep. With a last heave, Freddy pushed the tray to the stairs. He could hear Uncle Hotspur's heavy gasps only feet away.

"Batty, let's go!" he shouted.

With a mighty push, he sent the tray down the stairs and jumped on, clinging to his father's neck. Batty took a great leap and landed with a thump behind Freddy as the tray shot down the corkscrew stairs at breakneck speed. Halfway down they met a red-faced Uncle Hotspur. Before he could raise his gun, they crashed into him and he was bowled up into the air. He landed heavily across all three and joined them down the Slide of Doom.

"All hail the Plan Master!" Freddy laughed. He was almost squashed beneath the weight of his uncle.

"So, Flasheart, it is you," Sir Hotspur muttered into the wolf's ear, which was next to his mouth. The wolf gave a low, menacing growl. The tray sped faster and faster down the ancient steps as Freddy tried to reach his father's collar with the key.

"You'll wish you'd stayed in Coldfax, sir." Sir Hotspur fumbled with his gun, but Batty reached up and took his wrist in her jaws. Sir Hotspur gave a roar of anger. Flasheart snarled at his brother. They reached the foot of the stairs and sped along the corridor. Freddy at last managed to place the key in his father's padlock. It popped open.

Sir Hotspur finally shook Batty off. He grasped the padlock and tried to close it once again, just as the tray zoomed out into the courtyard and hit the fountain. Wolf, dog, boy, and man flew through the air and landed with one great splash in the ornamental pond. Once more the stone boy peed water onto Sir Hotspur's face. In Hotspur's left hand was Flasheart's Moonstone in its chain collar. The open padlock fell into the water and Hotspur looked around in fright. In the dark and heavy rain he couldn't make out where his brother was. As the thunder rolled above him, he held the Moonstone high.

"I order you to put this collar back on, sir," he roared into the night.

Suddenly a large human figure rose from the water.

"It's all over, Hotspur," a deep voice said. "You are undone."

"Dad!" Freddy spluttered, paddling over to hug his father.

"Not so, Flasheart. *You* are undone, sir!" Sir

Hotspur gave a cold laugh and took aim with his gun.

Hotspur pulled the trigger, but the wet gun didn't fire. Freddy gasped with relief as Sir Hotspur threw it away in disgust.

"You never frightened me before, Hotspur," Flasheart said calmly. "And you don't now."

"Nor me!" Freddy cried, but not so convincingly. A fork of lightning illuminated Flasheart's face. He had long black hair and a black beard, and his bright green eyes gleamed fiercely. All except Hotspur climbed out of the pond. Freddy watched another bolt of lightning hit the flagpole on top of his tower.

"Wow!" he yelped, but no one else seemed to notice. Batty stuck by Freddy's side, unsure who was friend and who was foe.

"I am the Grand Growler, and I command you to put on this collar," Sir Hotspur growled, once again holding the Moonstone high.

"Never!" Flasheart roared back.

"So I was right!" a new voice called. "At last I meet the Grand Growler."

All turned at the unpleasant surprise. There stood their greatest enemy.

CHAPTER TWENTY-ONE:
VICTORY?

Harriet and Chariot had slowly and cautiously
snuck down from the tower room. Unknown to
all, their round pink faces looked down into the
courtyard from the safety of the second floor.
They gave a gasp of fright as a flash of lightning
illuminated the wolf hunter's pale face. Cripp
walked toward the pond. He pointed a silver gun
directly at Sir Hotspur.

"Shouldn't we go and help?" Chariot wondered,
his eyes wide with fear. Harriet looked at him as
if he were mad.

"Do you want to be shot too, dunderbrain?" she
hissed.

"No." Chariot shrugged.

"Then keep quiet and watch."

* * *

The hunter pushed his greasy wet hair back onto his head. His thick glasses were spattered with raindrops.

"Get out of my castle if you want to live, sir," Sir Hotspur bellowed, stamping his foot in the pond.

Dr. Cripp ignored him. "I came here for two reasons," he sniggered revoltingly. "First, the Wolfen Names, which I have already found." He waved a small, very old red book inlaid with gold above his head in triumph. Freddy gasped. He must retrieve that book somehow.

"Second, I came to kill the Grand Growler. So shall I begin to rid Britain of Fangen forever." He cackled as madly as any wolf hunter ever had.

Sir Hotspur's face turned a ghastly shade of white. Flasheart began to step stealthily toward the doctor, while Freddy and Batty snuck backward into the gloom.

"But *he* is the Grand Growler, not I!" cried Hotspur, flinging his finger toward Flasheart. A fierce thunderclap crashed above them. "And that foolster is his son. Shoot them, not me!"

Dr. Cripp turned his gun on Flasheart.

"Traitor!" Freddy called. "It's not true."

"Oh yes, it is." Flasheart smiled charmingly.

"It *is*?" Dr. Cripp was puzzled.

"I am the true Grand Growler, but my *brother* there is a werewolf too."

"Don't be a fool, Flasheart," Hotspur called out desperately.

Dr. Cripp swung the gun back to him. "So you are both wolves?" He raised his eyebrows in alarm.

"Oh yes!" Flasheart continued with a happy smile. "How awful for you, Cripp."

"How so?" the doctor cried above the roar of the thunder, desperately swinging the gun to and fro. He was taking little notice of the boy and his dog.

"Well, if you shoot one of us, the other will have you in a second. You remember me, don't you? You see my scar, where you shot me? You escaped once, but only just. You won't again. I was so close I could smell your blood." Flasheart displayed his sharp teeth in a snarling smile.

"*You* are the wolf I shot?" Cripp croaked, shaking visibly with fear as he remembered that terrifying chase. "But you should have died."

"Shoot him again; he's the Grand Growler," Sir Hotspur called from the pond.

"Stay back," Dr. Cripp yelled desperately, unsure where to aim his silver gun.

Freddy saw his chance and flung himself onto the doctor's back, while Batty caught his trouser leg in her teeth and pulled hard.

"Release me, you monsters," Cripp cried in shock. His gun fired uselessly into the air as he tried to dislodge Freddy. Flasheart raced toward them, but Sir Hotspur jumped from the pond and grabbed his brother's leg. The two fell to the ground and rolled over in a snarling fury. Rain fell all around, and lightning arced almost into the courtyard.

Freddy stuck his fingers up Dr. Cripp's nostrils.

"Take that, you snotty toad," he said.

"Arrggh," the hideous man wailed.

Batty was still pulling at Cripp's trousers and managed to bring them down to his knees. Freddy rolled off as Cripp fell heavily onto his backside. The wolf hunter tried to pull up his trousers, but Batty wouldn't let go. Freddy tore off the doctor's glasses and threw them into the pond.

"You vile ruffian," Cripp cried, pointing the gun over his shoulder at Freddy. The boy grabbed his wrist and gave it a burn. He was incredibly good at them.

"Please, somebody help me," Cripp sobbed miserably. When nobody came, he had no option but to drop the gun. Freddy leaped down and grabbed it with relief.

"The Plan Master strikes again!"

Lightning struck the flagpole once again.

The sniveling doctor crawled away as fast as he could, but unfortunately, he had to leave his trousers behind, for Batty still held on to them tightly. Freddy laughed as he saw Dr. Cripp's spotty underpants disappearing into the gloom.

"So much for wolf hunters!" he called after him.

Mrs. Mutton was woken by the sound of gunshots.

"Burglars?" she wondered, and reached for the telephone next to her bed. "Yes, I need the police," she said urgently.

Freddy turned to see the two brothers still struggling. Uncle Hotspur held his father by the throat.

"I warned you to stay away, sir," he gasped into his brother's ear.

"This is my home, my family!" Flasheart grimaced.

Freddy fired a shot into the air. Uncle Hotspur looked up in surprise.

"You, *sir*, are a disgrace to werefolk," Freddy hissed, and aimed the gun at his uncle. Flasheart flung off his brother and stood up with a snarl.

"Freddy," Hotspur simpered, "what a *clever* boy. You see how my plan to distract Cripp has worked? I never meant him to harm you."

"If you have Sir Rathbone's blood in your veins, I'll eat my trousers. Eat 'em, sir!" Freddy cried. "With ketchup on!"

"Well done, Pinky." His father ruffled his hair. "I say, you've even found me some clothes." With a laugh, Flasheart pulled on Dr. Cripp's torn trousers. They were somewhat short for him, and he looked rather like a pirate.

"Dear boy, you're not going to shoot your favorite uncle?" Uncle Hotspur smarmed.

Freddy and Flasheart looked at each other.

"No, I'm going to shoot *you*," Freddy laughed.

"Flasheart, dearest brother . . . ," Sir Hotspur

cooed horribly. Freddy shuddered at his hypo-crisy.

"Put on your collar, Hotspur," Flasheart said coldly.

Sir Hotspur's eyes went wide with horror. "Not the Moonstone?" he gasped. "Am I never to be a wolf again, sir?"

"You're not fit to be a wolf," his nephew snorted.

"If it was good enough for Freddy, it's good enough for you," his brother growled. "You made your own punishment, Hotspur, now suffer it."

With a look of hatred, Sir Hotspur picked up the Moonstone's chain. He looked miserable indeed. His red mustache was drooping as the rain poured down his face. Sir Hotspur put the chain around his neck, and Flasheart threw the padlock through it. Freddy waved the gun again. With a snarl Hotspur closed the lock, and the chain was secure around his neck. Freddy had the key safe in his pocket.

"I shall have my revenge as wolf or man," Sir Hotspur vowed.

"Try telling someone who's interested, Hotspur," Flasheart said. "Now down to the dungeon until the Fang Council decides what to do with you."

Hotspur reluctantly began walking toward the door.

With a flash, a jagged fork of lightning zipped down. It struck the ground between Hotspur and the others, throwing them all down violently. Freddy gasped as the air flew out of him and the gun was flung from his hand. Batty barked urgently and licked his face.

"I'm all right, Batty. Dad, are you okay?" he croaked, sitting up. Flasheart was getting to his feet slowly.

"Just about, Pinky. Up you get." He hauled Freddy to his feet.

"Where's the gun?" Freddy looked around in concern.

They turned in time to see Sir Hotspur pick it up.

"Run, Freddy!" Flasheart cried. "He's dangerous."

Man, boy, and dog sprinted for the door that led to the tower passage.

When they were on the other side, Flasheart slammed it shut and locked it. "That was close," he said with relief, wiping the rain from his eyes.

Freddy looked through the keyhole.

"Hand over that key, sir, or I'll shoot," Hotspur yelled through the door.

"Never!" Freddy shouted back. "You locked up my dad, and now you'll pay for it."

Batty barked defiantly as the door rattled.

"No need to panic." Flasheart nodded. "The door will hold."

They heard Sir Hotspur running heavily across the courtyard.

"But the *other* door is wide open!" Freddy cried. "Can we panic now?"

"I insist on it," Flasheart cried. "Run!"

Dr. Cripp, meanwhile, had already started running by the time he left the courtyard.

"Wolves! Everywhere! Monsters!" he yelped as he made for the front door in his spotty underpants. The sooner he was safely outside the castle the better. He flung open the front door and ran out onto the wooden bridge, where he froze with fright.

Illuminated by a flash of light, he saw a hundred growling hounds guarding against his escape. Hamish's slower pack had arrived with reinforcements. The terrier recognized the man who had taken Batty. He remembered Freddy's instructions clearly: *Don't let anyone leave the castle!* The army of dogs bared their teeth.

"Oh my," wailed the pathetic man as Bruno and Hamish led the charge toward him. He turned tail and reached the castle in time to slam the door on the vicious horde. In desperation he began to look for somewhere to hide from the wolves within.

"Not up there, we'll be trapped," Flasheart cried as his son headed for the tower staircase. "To the kitchen."

Freddy nodded and ran in through the kitchen door.

"Freddy?" Mrs. Mutton cried. "And just where do you think you've been? Do you know how worried I've been?" She was standing in her dressing gown on a chair behind the door and holding a huge iron frying pan. She was waiting to ambush the burglars.

"Quick, he's after us!" Freddy hissed.

"Who is? Arrghh!" she cried. A large man with a black beard and long black hair had charged into the kitchen.

"No, not *him*," Freddy protested.

Too late.

With a loud, jarring bang, Mrs. Mutton brought her frying pan down upon Flasheart's head, and he slumped to the floor.

"She shoots, she scores," she laughed in triumph.

"Dad, Dad, wake up." Freddy shook his father urgently.

"Dad?" the old housekeeper climbed off her chair and bent down over the unconscious man. "*Flasheart?*" she cried, and nearly fell over. "But how?" She looked wonderingly at Freddy.

"No time to explain," he snapped. "But it was all my uncle's fault, and now he's on the rampage with a gun."

"I'll fire a silver bullet into your heart, sir," they heard Sir Hotspur roar. He was terrifyingly close.

"We'll see about that, Hotair," Mrs. Mutton whispered. "I'm ready to rumble." She held up her frying pan again.

"That won't stop him," Freddy whispered, looking down at his unconscious father. "I need to draw him away from Dad."

Just then they heard a tremendous clamor

echoing from the far side of the castle. They looked at each other in alarm.

Cripp had sneaked through the Great Hall to the far side of the castle. He quickly hid behind a curtain when he saw Sir Hotspur emerge from the door to the courtyard. The furious red-faced man stormed past and ran across the Great Hall, raging to himself. Cripp took his chance and rushed down the passage leading to the back of the castle. He saw Sir Hotspur's study and, next to that, the library. He made a dash . . . but he had forgotten about his trip wires. He fell and crashed into a suit of armor that stood nearby. In an instant Sir Hotspur, who had almost reached the kitchen, stopped, turned around, and raced back to the other side of the castle as fast as his fat would allow him. Cripp was flailing around on the floor among the armor.

"Oh my! Oh, mommy." The terrified hunter wept as he crawled away to the library.

With Batty at his heels, Freddy had run up the small servants' staircase from the kitchen. From the second floor he could look down across the courtyard and in though the windows diagonally opposite. He saw the doctor lock himself in the library just in time to avoid Sir Hotspur. The fallen suit of armor gave him an idea.

Without a second to spare he charged to the front of the castle, with Batty in hot pursuit. There at the top of the Red Stairs was Sir Rathbone's own suit of armor. In two minutes flat Freddy was wearing Sir Rathbone's heavy metal breastplate and helmet. The breastplate came down to his knees, and the helmet rattled loosely on his head. He reached up and grasped the huge sword and shield. With effort he lifted them and climbed onto the banister.

"Just let him try to shoot me now," he thought grimly.

"You're a traitor, Dripsy-Wimpsy!" Harriet's snide voice spoke out behind him.

Freddy jumped with fright. The twins had been watching him all this time.

"Yeah, you've betrayed the Grand Growler," her brother chimed in.

"Clear off, little piggies, this wolf is busy."

"You can't make us. And we are so going to tell. Everyone will know what a coward Freddy Lupin is." Harriet snorted.

Freddy ignored her. "Get out of my way, piggies, this is wolves' work." He nodded at Batty, who advanced toward the twins with a menacing growl. Freddy could hear Sir Hotspur hammering away below, trying to break into the library. Harriet suddenly gave a piercing scream as if she had been stabbed with a spear. Freddy jumped again.

All went quiet below, and then Sir Hotspur's heavy footsteps came toward the Great Hall. Harriet gave Freddy a smile of total evil.

"Now he's going to marmalize you into poodle jam," she laughed.

"We'll see about that," he snarled.

Freddy clamped down his visor. He wondered if Sir Rathbone had been this scared when he faced his foes. Summoning up his courage, he banged the sword on the shield and called out as loudly as he could, "I, Freddy Lupin, rightful heir to Sir Rathbone's glory, say this to you, Sir Hotair Catsvomit! I am going to kick your big, flabby bum!"

His words echoed around the castle as Uncle Hotspur rushed toward the Great Hall.

"Here goes nothing," Freddy said to himself,

feeling as if his stomach might actually explode with fear.

Sir Hotspur arrived red and panting. As he turned to face the stairs, he gave a startled jump.

With a blood-curdling yell, Freddy whizzed down the banister, sword held high. "Freddy the Fearless flies again," he called as he hurtled toward his uncle. Sir Hotspur instinctively bashed him away with his shoulder, and Freddy was bounced high into the air.

Then, a miracle! Or, more accurately, a *disaster*!

Freddy found he could fly. At least, that was how it felt. The back straps of his breastplate had caught on the huge chandelier that hung quite low from the ceiling. He was trapped swinging to and fro just above his uncle's reach.

"Whoops," he croaked. This was not part of the plan.

The twins gave a cheer of delight.

"What a dunderbrain!" Harriet shrieked.

"No foolster will stop me being a wolf!" Sir Hotspur said coldly, raising his gun. Batty was already on her way down the banister. She flew through the air and grabbed Sir Hotspur's wrist in her jaws. He gave a furious cry.

Freddy raised his visor. "Don't mess with my dog," he roared.

Sir Hotspur looked so fat and comical wrestling with the dog that Freddy couldn't resist pulling faces at him.

"Can't get me now, can you, Uncle Fart-Face?" he called. "Get his wobbly bum, Batty."

Sir Hotspur finally wrestled free of Batty and sent her skidding across the hall. He was now in an insane rage.

"First I will shoot you, sir, and then I'll turn you into dog poo and flush you down the lavatory!" he hissed. "But it's all over now. I shall be Grand Growler again, and you and Flasheart will be forgotten forever."

Sir Hotspur raised his gun for the last time.

"Oh, great howls," Freddy moaned in fear.

And then it happened.

The chain holding the chandelier could take the weight no longer and snapped with a sickening bang. Freddy was jolted off and plummeted with a yelp toward the floor—the chandelier following behind.

"Arrghh," he yelled helplessly. As he landed, his sword slammed onto the gun and shattered it. All around, bits of plaster debris and dust showered down. The dust cleared, and there sat Uncle Hotspur, his arms trapped tightly to his sides by the iron ring of the chandelier.

"The Champion!" Freddy roared, raising his arms in the air victoriously.

CHAPTER TWENTY-TWO:
THE PROPHECY

Mrs. Mutton and Flasheart appeared in the hall. Freddy's father had a large lump on his forehead. Batty limped over.

They laughed at the sorry sight of Sir Hotspur.

"Looks like the prophecy has come true." Flasheart smiled, looking at the sword and the shattered gun. "The legend always said that if the sword of Sir Rathbone was held by the hand of a true hero, it could save his werefolk from danger."

"That must make me a true hero, then." Freddy beamed.

"I suppose it must. Well done, Plan Master." Flasheart ruffled his son's pink hair. "No match for a pup, are you, Hotbot?"

"Who's been a naughty wolf, then?" Mrs. Mutton waggled her finger at the prisoner.

Sir Hotspur glared at them all.

"Release me this instant!" he bellowed, his red face and beard covered in plaster dust.

"No chance." Freddy snorted. He looked up to see if the twins were there, but they had snuck away. It looked like their days of power were ended.

They were interrupted by a loud bang on the front door. The police had arrived to investigate Mrs. Mutton's report of burglars. Using the point of Sir Rathbone's sword, Mrs. Mutton quickly led the protesting Hotspur down to the dungeon.

"Stop whining, Hotair." A prod with the sword was all the sympathy he got from her. "You're going to see my wooden spoon, I promise you that."

The policeman looked somewhat surprised when a small, pink-haired person wearing half a suit of armor answered the door.

"We had a phone call about some trouble, sir?" the policeman said, looking at the devastation in the hall with interest.

"No trouble that I know of, officer." Flasheart

beamed charmingly from behind Freddy. "Do you know of any trouble, Freddy?"

"No . . . except for that burglar we caught," Freddy piped up.

"Did we? Really?" Flasheart looked confused.

"Yes. If you'll just follow me, officer," Freddy said pompously as he led the way through the Great Hall.

"In there." He pointed at the library door.

The officer raised his voice. "This is the police. Open up."

They heard a scraping noise near the door.

"Have they gone? The werewolves?" came the whimpering voice of Dr. Cripp. "The castle is full of them."

The officer took a step back, a little embarrassed.

"I have to ask, sir. Do you know anything about werewolves?" He looked at Flasheart, who shook his head innocently.

"Oh yes, I do!" Freddy shouted eagerly, putting his hand up. "They have sharp teeth, suck blood, and turn into bats."

"No, no, I believe that is a vampire," the officer corrected.

"Surely you don't believe in vampires, officer?" Flasheart gave a chuckle. The officer turned red.

"Of course not! Not at all. It's all nonsense," he mumbled.

"Like werewolves, you mean?" Freddy asked with wide, innocent eyes.

"Yes, exactly," the officer agreed.

"Quite so," Flasheart continued. "So our burglar couldn't have seen one. Do you think he may be unbalanced?"

"Probably unhinged," the officer agreed.

"Totally barmy," Freddy concurerd.

Batty woofed.

The policeman spoke gently to Cripp through the library door. When he had at last persuaded him that there were no wolves in the castle, Cripp opened the door slowly.

"But there they are!" he screamed in terror when he saw the Lupins. "Wolves, they are all wolves."

"His mind has totally gone," the policeman tutted.

"So have his trousers," Freddy pointed out. "Totally gone."

The officer began to walk the poor, dazed Cripp to the main door.

"Just a minute," Freddy cried. He reached inside

the doctor's coat and extracted a red-and-gold book. Cripp flinched in terror as the boy gave a secret snarl. "He stole my book," Freddy explained, and put *The Red Book of Wolfen Names* safely behind his back.

"And what exactly has happened to your trousers, sir?" they heard the policeman ask as he left the castle. "It's not usual for men to walk around Milford in their underpants."

Batty ran onto the lawn and gave Hamish a signal that the men should be allowed to depart. The police car drove away, its occupants unaware that the eyes of a hundred hidden hounds watched them.

Freddy closed the door and then handed the book over to his father. "The Wolven Names are now safe with the Grand Growler once again," he said solemnly.

"Thanks to you, Freddy." Flasheart took the book with a smile and ruffled his son's pink hair. "The Plan Master."

You can well imagine the scenes that accompanied Freddy Lupin's arrival at the following month's Hidden Moonlight Gathering. His father was the Grand Growler once again, and Batty had been acclaimed as an honorary wolf. Best of all, Freddy's hair was now black again, the terrible pink dye having faded at last. He was cheered like a conquering hero by everybody except the Pukesome Twosome. They sat with bright green faces and hair, looking as sulky as you like. Freddy had had his revenge on them with permanent dye in their shampoo. No amount of scrubbing would remove it.

Sir Hotspur, still wearing the Moonstone and guarded by two large Weren, was forced to watch as his enemies were applauded. His red face sweated with frustration and fury.

Freddy took the stage. He was to have the honor of transforming first. Before the curtain was drawn back to reveal the full moon, Sir Grey Hightail, the leader of the Fang Council, spoke.

"This young pup has shown how a thirst for power led one of our greatest wolves astray. Whenever we think of your crimes, Hotspur, we should be humble. Thanks to Freddy, we have uprooted evil from our midst. Best of all, he has restored our brother Flasheart to his rightful place."

He was interrupted by much cheering. Flasheart, with his black hair trimmed and beard shaved off, grinned back and winked at his son.

"Hotspur," Hightail continued, "the Fang Council sentences you to wear that Moonstone and remain as a man for six years, to match the time you locked your brother in darkness."

Sir Hotspur went pale with horror. To be deprived of being a wolf was the greatest punishment for werefolk. Hotspur's disgrace was complete. But Hightail had not finished.

"We cruelly turned away this pup, but he did not turn his back on us. He showed us the true meaning of the Pact of the Fangen. He has foiled the dreaded Cripp and proven himself the savior of all Wolfenkind." Hightail held *The Red Book of Wolfen Names* aloft for all to see.

"A wolf shall never again be judged by his species, but by his actions. Freddy Lupin, you stand side by side with Sir Rathbone as our greatest heroes." The werefolk cheered madly. Sir Hotspur looked sick with hatred.

"Well, perhaps I'm the second-greatest hero ever . . . Sir Rathbone is still the best," Freddy said generously.

The crowd cheered as Freddy, his heart bursting with pride, stood up to transform.

"They really won't mind that I'm going to be a poodle?" he checked with his father.

"Not one bit." Flasheart winked.

His father pulled back the heavy curtain. There in the sky shone the full moon.

"Now is the Grand Growling and High Howling of the Hidden Moonlight Gathering of Werefolk. We howl thanks for the ancient magic of the Moonstone. Now, by the power of the silver moon, let the Transwolfation begin!" cried Flasheart.

As the warmth of the moonbeams fell onto Freddy, he dropped to his hands and knees and felt his blood heating. His skin crept all over like a hundred scabs falling off. Again he felt the searing shiver as the hair grew through his skin. With a final shake, he put back his head to bark.

"*Hooowwlll,*" came a deep noise from his throat.

Like the time before, cries of astonishment filled the Great Hall. Freddy guessed something was not quite right.

"Oh, now what?" he cried, rushing to the window. In it he saw his reflection: a young, strong black wolf.

"I'm a wolf!" he laughed in amazement. "At last, I'm a wolf. . . . How?"

The hall filled with cheers and howls.

That night, when he led the Blood Red Hunt next to his father, Freddy was the happiest wolf alive. He hardly knew how he deserved it, but he could only be grateful, because his every dream had come true.

POSTSCRIPT

Of course, this is real life and not fantasy, and Freddy's story does not have a dream ending. As the months passed, he found that he didn't always transform into a wolf. Dripsy-Wimpsy was as much a part of him as ever. On each full moon, Freddy could never tell whether he would transform into poodle or wolf, but whatever he was he walked with pride.

He and Batty became inseparable after she moved into Farfang Castle. Freddy could be just as annoying and silly as ever, especially now that he was a *hero*, but she loved him still. They were never happier than when racing through the woods whenever the full moon shone.

Sir Hotspur was banished to Dundaggard

Castle in the very northernmost part of Scotland. There Laird McDaggard, a member of the Fang Council, guarded him. Hotspur spent his days pacing the courtyard and nights staring at the moon, and always, always, vowing revenge on Freddy Lupin.

Harriet and Chariot accompanied their father to Scotland. They were not in the least bit pleased to be living with Laird McDaggard and his wife in the middle of nowhere. Their behavior there was so atrocious that they were soon sent away to a strict school. You'll be happy to hear that they were very miserable there indeed.

After seeing that Freddy and Batty were safe, Hamish, Bruno, and the other dogs disappeared into the night, back to the Wildside. They would often turn up at the kitchen door looking for sausages and were always welcomed as friends when they did. Bruno turned up most often, for no matter where he roamed, he just never met another mongrel with eyes as pretty as Batty's.

Coldfax Fort soon fell into disrepair without Mayor Lupin to keep it open. When the Commander searched, not a single dog remained, not even Cerberus. Where he had gone was a mystery. But the wolfhound had discovered how to move the grate and explore the drains, and no one ever checked down there. It was said that despite the disappearance of the dogs, the ghost hound remained, for at night his howls could be heard coming from somewhere in that terrible place.

And Dr. Cripp?

He is now in a special hospital for the completely confused. He is happy to tell all the doctors who visit him that the country has been taken over by werewolves. The doctors will make sure that he's never allowed out, for he is quite mad, you know. . . .

Werewolves? Who ever heard of anything as crazy as that?